First Dog

Nikos Kavvadias

First Dog

Translated from the Greek
with an introduction and glossary
by

Simon Darragh

Shoestring Press

Typeset and Printed by Q3 Print Project Management Ltd, Loughborough (01509 213456)

Published by Shoestring Press
19 Devonshire Avenue, Beeston, Nottingham, NG9 1BS
Telephone: (0115) 925 1827
www.shoestringpress.co.uk

First published 2002
Translation © Simon Darragh
© Copyright: The Estate of Nikos Kavvadias
ISBN: 1 899549 73 0

east midlands
arts
making creative
opportunities

Shoestring Press gratefully acknowledges financial assistance from East Midlands Arts and the Hellenic Foundation of London, without whom the publication of this book would have been impossible.

Acknowledgements

The core work of this translation – the writing of the first, unreadable, draft – was started and completed during a fellowship at Hawthornden Castle in June 1998. I am grateful to all who made this possible and enjoyable, especially Drue Heinz and Adam Czerniawski.

As with *Wireless Operator*, my previous volume of Kavvadias translations, Alan Ross was a staunch support.

I thank also the International Writers' and Translators' Centre of Rhodes, during a stay at whose premises in, appropriately enough, the old British Admiralty building, I worked on the final draft of this translation.

Alex Watson, who donated the ancient AppleMac computer I use, performed the miracle of rescuing both book and machine when it deleted "First Dog" in its entirety during a breakdown.

Innumerable Greek friends and brief acquaintances have helped with obscure words and phrases, sometimes in unlikely and non-literary circumstances.

Translator's Preface

There is a story that the translators who made the King James Bible were locked in separate rooms to do their work, and all came up with exactly the same result. Pious beliefs apart, even those who have never thought deeply about translation, who will happily talk of a "faithful" version without stopping to consider what a multitude of sins – or goodnesses – the word may cover, must see that the story can't be true. There are as many translations, even of a short work, as there are translators.

Given that one can't reproduce "everything" – a photocopy of the original would be unhelpful to the foreign reader – translators have to make decisions. A translator of Swinburne into French might decide, as many English readers have, that sense is less important than sound, and sacrifice the one to save the other. Conversely in the unlikely event of a felicity of style being discovered in the instruction book for a German washing-machine, its English translator might ignore it in favour of clarity of "sense"; a term less slippery in washing-machines than in poetry.

What about a novel? Specifically, an autobiographical novel, by a poet and sailor, about life in the Greek Merchant Marine. What should be preserved, and what sacrificed? One extreme might be to turn it into a story about English sailors; to find English equivalents not just for nautical terms, but for Greek sailors' conversations; to consider what English sailors might say in similar circumstances. (Whatever they might be – perhaps one should translate the circumstances too?) That would be to lose the specifically Greek character of the book in favour of something the English reader would find more familiar and easier to read, or at least as easy to read as the original is for a Greek reader. There is a defensible sense in which such a translation would be "faithful".

At the other extreme is the so-called "literal" translation; actually impossible because, whatever dictionaries may say, no two languages can be mapped, word by word, onto each other. To suppose that they can be is to confuse languages with cyphers. For instance, the dictionary tells us that the Greek word *magazi* "means" shop. But a betting-shop is not, even in Greece, a magazi, and a Greek restaurant, though a magazi, is not a shop. Well, "As literal as possible", then. (Something translators are often asked for.) The result would indeed, though in English words, be all Greek to the reader.

I have, of course, gone to neither extreme, though I have, in different places, approached both. In short, I have been deliberately inconsistent in my decisions. Where characters have called each other by a word that translates literally as "baby" I have usually used "idiot" or "boy", on the grounds that they were calling each other "baby" in circumstances in which an English sailor might call another "idiot" or "boy", rather than those in which he might call him "baby". But there is an occasion when a sailor from the Black Sea calls his companions "Carthaginian Buffaloes" and I have given this literally: it would be a shame to lose it, however rarely the expression might be heard among English speakers.

I have, then, made different decisions in different places, in order to preserve what, in each particular case and in my judgement, seemed more valuable or interesting to the English reader, though the overriding consideration has always been what will give the best idea of what Kavvadias wrote.

Every language has culture-specific words that can only be translated by a clumsy paraphrase. For instance, the Greek and Turkish sweet called loukoumas (not the same as loukoumi) has no English equivalent; Greek/English dictionaries usually give "A kind of doughnut", and indeed at a snack bar in a fishing village I know there is a sign for foreigners, offering "Lemonade", "Nes-coffee", "Cheese Pie", and "A kind of doughnut". Similarly Pring, in his obscurantist *Oxford Dictionary of Modern Greek*, gives for "Bouzouki" "A kind of mandoline", which is not only unhelpful but inaccurate: the bouzouki belongs to an entirely different family of instruments to the mandolin. (Only those who approach popular music with the amused disdain of a high court judge peering over his spectacles to enquire "Who is Diana Dors?" spell it with a final "e".)

Such culture-specific words are usually best left merely transliterated, with an explanatory note. This is what I have done in *First Dog*, but rather than pepper the text with footnotes, which in a translation give at least the appearance of copping-out, I have confined my explanations to a glossary at the back, in which I have also included some nautical terms, and partial explanations of the more puzzling (to an English reader) Greek customs.

This book will sometimes not "Read like English"; something translations are often expected to do, though one wonders why. The story is not English, the sailors are not English, they are Greek, and most of them Kephallonians to boot. Many Greek readers have difficulties with the original of *First Dog*; parts of it "Don't read like Greek", just as some English works don't read like English on their first appearance: if we were to discover tomorrow that Hopkins's *The Windhover* or Woolf's *The Waves* had in fact been translations from the Chinese and the French, some of us might well say they must be "bad" translations, because they "Don't read like English". I daren't compare my translation to the works of Hopkins or Woolf, but its English is no stranger than theirs.

A few specific points: the heirarchy of the Greek Merchant Marine doesn't correspond to that of the British. I have translated the Greek Δόκιμος as "Cadet" or "Deck Apprentice". These are recognized positions in the British Merchant Marine, whereas the usual translation, "Midshipman", is a rank that exists only in the Royal Navy. I have constantly referred to the character Yerasimos as "First Mate", but this is an approximation: he has many, but not all, of the rights and responsibilities of an English First Mate, and he has others that a First Mate does not. The Greek name for his rank translates literally as "Grammarian"; not a common post on an English ship.

Lower ranks usually address all officers as "Captain-" followed by the officer's first name. Thus our hero the wireless officer is usually called "Captain Nikos". The "real" Captain rarely appears; he is usually refereed to (not in his presence) by a word that translates literally as "The Brute".

There are a few short passages – one at least apparently describing unusual sexual practices – which I cannot claim to understand completely, nor can even my most sophisticated Greek friends. I have translated these as literally as I can.

In at least two passages people are recognized as being from Kephallonia by their bizarre, but presumably typical, imprecations. The expressions they use come as near as anything can to being untranslatable; my English versions are, I think, no more or less bizarre to English ears than the originals are to non-Kephallonian Greek ears.

Simon Darragh

First Dog

To Panayis Yiannoulatos

FERDINAND: Is she dead?

BOSOLA: She is what you would have her.
               Fix your eye here.

FERDINAND: Constantly.

BOSOLA: Do you not weep?
               Other sins only speak; murder shrieks out.
               The element of water moistens the earth.
               But blood flies upward and bedews the heavens.

FERDINAND: Cover her face; mine eyes dazzle; she died young.

Webster, the Duchess of Malfi

Part 1

"Who is it?"

A hand appeared, lifting the hook from the outside, and the door half-opened. "It's me, Captain Yerasimos, the cadet. Can I talk to you? Were you sleeping?"

"What the devil d'you want? We were up there for four hours, couldn't you have thought of it before? Come on in then, and put the door back on the hook."

The First Mate of the *Pytheas* – in his forties, dark, with big eyes – was sitting in his underwear on a revolving chair which was screwed to the deck. He had one leg up on the other and was rubbing his ankle; his body shone with sweat.

"So, boy. Anything happening up there?"

Diamantis, the deck-apprentice – tall, blond – stood awkwardly in the doorway, wiping his forehead with his left hand. He was obviously embarrassed.

"Well – Captain Yerasimos – I don't know – I think I've got something."

"Where, boy?"

"You know, down there – like a boil – not very big, and it doesn't hurt, but I don't know –"

"You need a shave, boy." He drummed his fingers on the edge of the desk. "Go and get the wireless officer. If he's asleep wake him up."

"What about the –?"

"Just do as I say."

Alone again, the First Mate wiped his neck with a khaki handkerchief. The cabin was two metres by three with a porthole above the bunk. A desk, a sofa, a shelf with a few books. On the bulkhead, a brass oil-lamp in gimbals. A fan stirred the hot air.

The electric light was flickering; he got up and turned it off. Faint streaks of eastern light could be seen through the porthole. He tore a page from an old copy of *Brown's Almanac* and emptied the ash-tray onto it. Screwing it into a ball he aimed it at the open porthole and missed; dog-ends spattered over the bunk. "I'll shit in your hands," he muttered.

As he was scooping up the mess the door-hook lifted again and the Wireless Operator came in. Below average height, thinning hair, khaki trousers held up only by the top button. One of his ears stuck out, bigger than the other. "Morning," he said; "What's going on?"

"I wish something *was* going on. This young idiot thinks he's caught a dose. Take a look, will you? You know about these things."

Diamantis was standing in the corner, head hanging, like a figure by Donatello. The wireless officer sat down on a little folding stool. "Drop them," he said.

"Me?" The boy looked confused.

"Oh, come on, who? There are no girls here. Come a bit closer. Captain Yerasimos, plug that lamp in and shine it on his legs. In fact put all the lights on. That's better – now. When did you last go with a woman?"

"Just over a month ago, in Algiers, when we were taking on coal."

"And when did you first notice this?"

"Two nights ago, just after we left Sabang."

"Did you put anything on it?"

"Iodine."

"O.K. Take off your vest, your trousers, and your pants."

"Everything?"

"Like the day your mother bore you."

The flickering electric light showed the boy's body dead white from the waist down. The wireless officer looked at his chest, stomach, legs. "How old are you?"

"Seventeen – just."

"Many happy returns. Tell me, Diamantis, was she black?"

"Yes."

"Beautiful?"

"Very."

"In a brothel?"

"No. I was going up the alleys towards the Casbah. I was on my way to Red Sea Road, to get a bracelet for my sister. This girl called me from a doorway, 'Esma – Taale,' and I went in. Just like that, quickly, we didn't even get as far as the bed. D'you think I've caught something?"

"Oh, come on, relax. Don't pick at it, just cover it with a bit of cotton-wool soaked in salt water. Hot camomile at night. And wash your hands properly. Yerasimos, when do we get to Santoun?"

"Another six days at least."

"Mm. Tell me, boy, does it hurt?"

"No, just a twinge now and then."

"Headache?"

"No – yes, after lunch yesterday. Like something pressing on my temples. What would that be?"

"Nothing, go to bed. Do what I said, and when we put in, straight to the doctor. The usual thing."

Diamantis left without a word. They listened to his footsteps echoing across the deck. The First Mate got up, unplugged the lamp and put it back on the desk. "The mule, the son of a whore. Did you hear? He went up the hill for a *bracelet*. I was supposed to be watching out for him. We were worn out with work that day. Can't understand how he managed to slip away."

"Got any matches?" asked the Wireless Officer. "Just a handful. Thanks." He got up to go.

"Don't go yet, have a drink. Kirsch?"

"No, I don't drink."

"Whisky, brandy?"

"Nothing."

"So you've given it up altogether? Difficult."

"It's three years now." But the Wireless Officer's eye fell on a bottle on the glass shelf over the wash-basin. He went over, put a little in a glass, and added a few drops of water. The drink clouded.

"I'll have the same," said the First Mate quietly. The Wireless Officer got him a drink without speaking, then downed his own in one gulp. He coughed a little, then said "D'you remember, Yerasimos?"

3

"Yes."

"Well I'll remind you anyway. It's all of eighteen years ago. On that island in the gulf. We got away from the Captain around midday, just like that Diamantis you were cursing a moment ago. Blind drunk. We managed to find the village with the black girls, and you laughed at the notice, 'Supplying of intoxicants to natives is strictly forbidden.' We had a couple of bottles each hidden on us; cheap whisky. Then I found the other notice someone had left, 'Beware of native women. All rotten here.' That's when the English Sally Army girls bumped into us. One tall, old, and skinny, with rotten teeth, and the other one young, with green eyes. The old one was furious; 'Where are you going?' she said.

" 'To the women.'

" 'Shame on you. Go back to your ship.'

" 'We'll go back' – I can't remember which of us said it – 'We'll go back, but only if you two come with us.' And it was you who poked your middle finger up in the air.

"Well the old girl spat at us through her broken teeth; 'Hell damn you both, dirty dogs.' I'll swear the young one was giggling.

"So off we went to the black girls in their bamboo huts. Naked, just strips of coloured rag in their hair. The smell of them! We couldn't keep our hands off them. Funny little tits, like rubber. Then we swapped over for a second go.

"Must have been about three weeks later, in the Bay of Biscay, that it first showed itself. After that we – lost track of each other –"

Captain Yerasimos shut him up with a wave of his hand. He took out a packet of English cigarettes. As they were lighting up he leant over and said "Show me your hand. The right one. Go on, open it."

Puzzled, the Wireless Officer showed his palm.

"Ah, look. See? Stupid. Like kids."

There was a thin white line on the Wireless Officer's hand, from the thumb to the wrist.

"I wish it had never happened," said the First Mate.

"Are we going to rake all that up now, at dawn? I'd forgotten all about it."

"But *I* haven't. It gets to me sometimes at night, on watch. It was in Huelva, if you remember – that heathen gypsy woman, barefoot, dusty feet, sweat like fermenting wine. It was you she fancied – and I went and pulled out that knife, the one you'd sharpened for me yourself only three hours before on the engine-room stone. And you went and grabbed the blade.

"And now, here we are again. I could have shit myself when I saw you coming up the gangplank in Port Said. Since then I've been hoping for a chance to talk; d'you still hold it against me?"

"Come on, Yerasimos, don't be an idiot. Tell me, what became of the last Wireless Officer?"

"Went off his head, poor sod. He was terrified of the sharks. 'Don't throw the left-overs in the sea,' he used to tell the sailors, 'you're attracting the cuckolds, they're surrounding us.' Then it turned out he had cramp in his hand; couldn't transmit properly. Couldn't hold the key the right way; burnt out the contacts. At Christmas he pulled the set out onto the hatches and took it all to pieces. Right out in the open sea he had the aerial taken down, to polish it – you people all go crazy in the end. You changed the subject. Let me finish. Anyway I jumped ship the night I cut you. Got a place on a Spanish ship. But they sent my papers on, all clear, no charge against me. Well?"

The Wireless Officer smiled. "I hadn't forgotten. But actually you did me a favour. You're strong in the arm and twice my size. If it had come to blows one of us would have been killed, and no prizes for guessing which."

They sat looking at the floor for a while, saying nothing.

"D'you still paint?" the First Mate asked. "I remember you were crazy about it. You'd even pick up bits of coal and draw on all the white bits of the ship till the bosun caught you at it."

"Not any more."

"Why not?"

"Well, I lost a couple of colours – the greens – and then –"

"So," Yerasimos interrupted, "what about that boy?"

"Diamantis? As soon as we put in we'll send him off to the doctor. If he tests positive we'll pepper his arse with bismuth and penicillin. What about you, did you get over it all right?"

"Oh, yes. The usual drugs for four years, and then a load more of the new ones. You?"

"I was ill for two years. I'm not sure which was worse, the illness or the treatment, they both drive you crazy. Strange sickness. As long as you have the boils, you think you're rotting, that you stink, that your nose is going to drop off any minute. Then when they clear up, you forget all about it. But for the rest of your life you torture yourself. The slightest headache, a little pimple, a bit of dizziness, and you're scared shitless for months. Is it like that for you?"

"It was, but I laughed it off. I think I'm all right now. Good stuff, the new drugs."

"I don't believe anything kills it. There was this Chinese sailor in Chingtao. He said 'You know why they use four different drugs? Because the worm gets used to the first one, and eats it up. Same with the second, then it gets full up with the third, and falls asleep with the fourth. But it doesn't die; it just sleeps.' I believe that, whatever they say. The best medicine is the heat. That's why I prefer tropical passages. Have you seen the blacks in Jamaica, Port Sudan, Bousin? Legs all scarred, but no open wounds, no noses eaten up. They die of old age. It's better in the tropics. I feel sorry for that boy, he seems a decent enough lad. Are you supposed to be looking after him?"

"Actually the Captain is. He's his uncle. The boy's mother's a widow, and there are sisters too. They're waiting for him, he's the breadwinner now. If his uncle finds out about this there'll be trouble."

"So what's the Captain like?"

"About as much use as a castrated bull. Seems to follow your theory as far as illness goes. In the Red Sea he sleeps under woollen blankets. He's got an electric fire and he keeps it on in all weathers."

"But a good sailor?"

"I wouldn't trust him to poke his own eyes out, the mule."

"Is he a Kephallonian, at least?"

"No idea. He's married to the owner's sister, get the picture? He doesn't need to know one side of the bridge from the other, he just sends the steward to me with his orders. Have you never spoken with him?"

"Not really. He came to the door of the wireless cabin the other day. 'You'll catch something,' he said, 'you've got the fan blowing right on your back.' Asked me if I happened to have the last issue of *Treasures*. Said I hadn't and he left. I noticed his clothes stank of medicine – listen, I'm keeping you up. I've got to go and disconnect the batteries anyway; cheers."

"Come on up next time I'm on watch, if you feel like it. We'll talk over old times."

After a little while the electric light went out by itself. The First Mate loosened the waistband of his trousers and lay on his back on the sofa. He pushed off his shoes and they clattered onto the deck. A quarter to six, local time, by the clock.

The *Pytheas*, five-thousand ton standard-class cargo vessel, dating from the First War, fitted with tanks and a reciprocating engine, was sailing seven miles off Singapore. A depressing, sickly light, like dirty oil, spilt through the portholes.

First Watch

"Don't fight it, see? You keep twisting it one way and the other, that's why it's pulling. We've wasted an extra ton of coal this watch with your bad steering. I've told you so many times, treat the wheel gently. Now if there's a current, that's a different matter."

"I can't help it, Captain Yerasimos. It just doesn't want to steer for me."

"You'll just have to learn helmsmanship, Polychroni – where's Diamantis?"

"Er – gone to read the log," the boy murmured evasively.

"Who sent him? What log?"

"Don't know."

"So it's left to us two, eh?" He lifted his binoculars and leant on the rail. "From where you're steering, can you make out the green light O.K.?"

"Yes."

"Right. Keep on that course, don't change direction at all."

"Right you are."

The Wireless Officer came quietly up the companionway. "I sent you up the weather report a little while ago."

"Yes, thanks. Something happening in the Hong Kong area, off the headland?"

"We're a long way off yet. We'll see later –"

"All in good time. Tell me, d'you ever sleep?"

The Wireless Officer shrugged. "An hour or two in the afternoon, same around dawn."

"So little?"

"For years on the mailboats I had the worst watch, the twelve to four. We never changed. I've lost the taste for sleep. You wake up, and you can't get off again –"

Diamantis crept up the companionway like a thief, buttoning his trousers. He spat out his cigarette, stamped on it, and pushed his way into the wheelhouse.

"The mails? Tell me about them," said the First Mate.

"Crowds, noise, putting in to port every day. Crew of ten. The passengers get on your nerves; couples hanging around outside your cabin, not a moment's peace. You've got a cabin and you haven't."

"How d'you mean?"

"Well, where can the deck-class passengers sleep? The number of times I've had to sleep in a chair! Were you never on the mails?"

"Once. For six months. But I paid for it."

"Tell me."

"Later; carry on."

"Passengers. Worst cargo you can have. Worse than minerals, worse even than linseed. Travel with your best friend, might be your brother, do anything for him, but as soon as you reach his port, you lose him. Not even a goodbye, he just forgets. Forgets! Can you credit it?"

"Might not be to blame; might have had problems."

"All that shit from the passengers, 'When will we get there? What time exactly? Will it be rough? Have you had a storm report?' Petty, pathetic. And the mail workers. Such children! Putting their best suits on three hours before you make land. Like crows on the rail, waiting for carrion. And if there's an orphan girl travelling alone, woe betide her! Like a lamb to the slaughter."

"Just a moment. Diamantis!"

The cadet put his cigarette out and came over.

"I've told you not to smoke on watch. Take the Aldis and signal to that tramp-steamer for name and destination. Slowly, so they can read you."

The First Mate turned back to the wireless officer. "Well, what did you do then?"

"I was fed up with the Med. I got on a big ship on the Australia run. Genoa, Porto, Aden, Colombo, Fremantle, Melbourne. Thirty-three day journey. Good seas to travel on. You should see the immigrants coming aboard in Genoa. Loudspeakers blaring in five languages, crazy mixture of people, all colours. Each with their own religion, but all of them lost, without what you'd really call faith. All off to try again, you see. Some of the men still with their call-up papers on them. Women who'd go with you for a cigarette or a drink, or for nothing, just because they're fed up with always saying no.

"I remember I fell asleep when we finally got there, and when I woke they'd all disappeared into the freezing fog of the Yara-Yara river. Where was all the noise, the murmuring that had lulled me to sleep all those nights, that I'd got so fed up with, that I'd loved? The deck was a desert of broken chairs, old newspapers in all languages, Jewish books, combs, empty envelopes – and the people? All swept away, gone."

"I can imagine what you did with the Jewesses. I bet you had a good time."

The wireless officer lit a match and held it high, as if to see the First Mate's face by its little flame, and let it go out without lighting a cigarette. "No. Never at sea. Twenty years on the ships, but I never took one into my bunk. I'm like a dog in a manger. If there was one I liked, and she wanted it, we waited until we made port, and went to a hotel. Never on board."

"Silly ideas. All you people who work in wireless cabins are a bit crazy; the electricity does something to your heads. What made you choose wireless officer anyway? You were aiming for master's papers."

"I wasn't really aiming for anything. I just wanted to travel. The others who started with us got their papers in four years. You too. But I liked the fo'c'sle. Oh, there were plenty of Greek captains who tried to help me, and plenty who took the piss or gave me the five fingers. It hurt my pride. I did study for second mate's papers, but then I met a relative of my mother's who was a shipowner. He was the only person who understood, and he always had a job for me, no questions asked. I told him the way I felt. 'Become a wireless officer,' he said. 'Better a wrecked wireless cabin than a fo'c'sle no-one can manage.' I drank then, you see. What about you, did you get your master's papers?"

"No, not yet. Not sure I ever will."

"Why on earth not? There aren't many know the job as well as you do."

"No, it's not true. I'm not worth – don't you know? Did you never hear the story?"

"No?"

"Well, hear it now. I did my full time at sea towards second mate, took my papers and went to work on the cargo-ships. Two years more and I was due for First Mate, but I hadn't taken the exams. So off I went again for another two and a half years. I was going to take the papers in another six months.

"Now I was a bit short of money and I fancied making some. Not so as to cut a fine figure, just so's to have something in my pocket. Well a distant relative fixed me up with a job as acting First Mate on a mailboat. I was just like you; the mails disgusted me. We were on the Alexandria – Piraeus – Brindisi run. I got a bit clever, and started to make a little money on the side. Might be fillet steak, or a silk dress, or lighter flints and cigarette papers. Smuggling's not really a crime; you put your money down, you buy, you don't steal. I wouldn't handle drugs though, my pride revolted at that. But why worry about things that don't hurt anyone, I thought. I used to make two or three thousand drachmas every trip; lot of money in those days. In three months I had more than enough to stop work and go and study for the exams. And then there was the little building plot in Athens to see to. Not much, but I thought 'A roof over her head for the old lady, so she isn't out in the rain in her old age.' You remember my mother?"

"Yes. We ate at your place once. I remember you killed a chicken. We drank Kephallonian wine and got pissed, and started eyeing up that girl your mother'd brought from the village."

"Angelika!"

"That's the one. Like loukoumi. But your mother was cunning, she sent her off to do the dishes, the crafty old thing."

"That's right. Anyway, a month before I left the ship I had twenty thousand. One last go, I thought, and I bought everything. In three days I had ten times as much. Well when I went home with all that money the old girl smelt a rat. 'May the Lord have mercy on your soul,' she said, 'and on your father's, on the seas where he travels, far from your dirty work,' and she threw me out on the street.

"So of course I went back on board. We came back from Alexandria one Thursday morning, and there I was, past the customs, with the stuff safe, standing outside St Nicholas' church, where I'd stopped to get my breath back. 'So much for poverty,' I thought.

"To this day I still can't work out how I found myself inside, at midday, sentenced to eighteen months. Who had I hurt? Was it a set-up? An informer? – Jealousy! I hadn't thought of that. Now I was finished, all washed up. I had twenty-five drachmas in my pocket, and my mother was looking after the thousands. Brave lady. Like a rock, I tell you.

"The screws smiled as they locked me up. Black smiles, but smiles. They let my mother in to see me once a week. She never reproached me. 'Courage, my boy! It's something you have to get through, then you'll come out and we'll forget all about it.'

"How she stood it I never asked, and I'll never know. One Sunday in winter she turned up at midday carrying a little canteen. Sweating, red in the face, in her old black dress and dusty worn-out shoes. 'I brought you your favourite food,' she says; 'boiled chicken. Eat it now, don't let it get cold.'

"'Listen, mother,' I said, 'We'll eat together. And I want to know why you came on foot, otherwise I won't eat a mouthful.'

"She got wild. 'You've got it all wrong, my boy. I ate this morning. I came here on the tram, you think I'd come on foot? Don't be silly.'

"I'm sure it was the first time she'd ever lied to me. It was a whole chicken, except for the head and feet, she'd brought. As she got up to go, she put a twenty drachma piece and five cheap cigarettes in my hand. 'I'll be here again on Thursday, my boy. It's a holiday, they're bound to let me in. Just keep your spirits up.'

"I watched through the bars as she went off, all bent over. I shouldn't have looked. I saw her trip and fall on her knees. Well there were some kids playing on the street, and one little bastard, some son of a whore, about eight years old, comes up behind and pushes her over. I turned away; I couldn't look. When I turned back she'd gone round the corner; the little sods were still laughing.

"A few days later the governor sent for me. I was worried sick. 'Er – we're all human,' he said carefully; 'we all end up in the same place –'

"Somehow I managed to ask who'd buried her. 'Well the council of course. Who else?'

"When I came out of prison there wasn't so much as a saucepan left in the house.

"I took ship on the Panama canal run. Came back three years later and took her bones back to the village. Got her a marble stone and put pots of flowers in front of it – she loved flowers.

"It's eleven years now since she went. Just a poor woman from Kephallonia. Since then I can't bring myself to touch a child. I don't even give my nephews and nieces sweets. Only kicks, when I get the chance. Evil creatures, children."

He turned to look at the wireless officer, but found he'd gone down the companionway without a word.

"Diamantis, time to check the log and change watch."

A yellow dawn, and the First Mate's face yellow as a beeswax candle.

Second Watch

"Why are you looking so sorry for yourself, boy?"

"It's my head, Captain Yerasimos, it's splitting. Like someone's stabbing me just over the right eye."

"It's the heat. I've got it too. Take an aspirin; it'll go."

"I've taken three since this morning; they don't do anything. And there's something else: my hair's coming out in handfuls when I comb it."

"Did you see the wireless officer?"

"I passed by the wireless cabin just now, but he's working. If only I knew what I've got –"

"Whatever you've got, we're headed for port. You'll survive. It's like a furnace tonight – not a breath of wind anywhere – ah, there you are, Nikos. Polychronis, go and make two coffees with a little sugar. So, how's your watch been?"

"Dreadful. The receiver's boiling with atmospherics and the wireless cabin's like an oven. Whatever you touch you burn yourself. And they've shut off the fresh water. Now the bad news: there's a typhoon on the way, I sent you the report."

"Don't worry, we're a long way off yet. And the way it looks now it'll probably break up; we won't feel it. You're not worried, are you?"

"That sort of thing doesn't bother me. I don't give a damn if I drown. The only thing I'm afraid of is illness."

Diamantis crept closer to listen.

"And women," the wireless officer continued.

The First Mate laughed; "If you don't get over the one, why worry about the other?"

"That's not what I mean. It's death-beds I'm afraid of. With this sort of sickness, that still lets you travel –"

"Speak a bit lower; there's a little night-bird listening. What were you saying about women?"

"It's true; I'm afraid of them."

"We all are, more or less. The ones in harbour towns anyway."

"They're the best. No-one ever caught anything in a brothel, everyone knows they're clean, the girls all wash as soon as they finish work – I remember one I went with in Las Vegas. I took off my shirt. My vest was torn, in rags. Well I got hold of her and she said 'Slow down, what's your hurry?' Then she dragged my vest off and started patching it. Later, when I tried to pay her, she blushed like a schoolgirl. 'If that's all you've got, keep it. You can bring me some of those nice Greek raisins if you ever come this way again.' Well I showed her I'd got plenty of money on me. 'In that case,' she said, 'do me a favour, buy yourself a new vest. If your mother could see you now she'd weep.' See what I mean? It's the others that scare me, the fine ladies who don't do it for money, the ones who can read and write. The ones we marry."

"Don't you want to get married?"

"No. Miserable seamen. I've seen their wives go down to the quay, long before the ship's due in, and stand waiting under the midday sun, or in the pouring rain. I've seen them waving goodbye as the ship casts off: tortured, worn out with abortions, a string of howling kids hanging on their skirts. They're – unfulfilled, if you see what I mean. The man's not there. Any crafty sod can get off with them easily, and the cuckolds can go and drown. I know many a sailor who's caught something from his own wife. Marriage? Forget it."

"You're wrong," Yerasimos said, shaking his head slowly. "You're always telling the same old story. There are thousands of good ones, who bless the bread they eat. Alone when they give birth, alone at the baptism, and alone when they're buried. But if we're away for five, ten years, what d'you expect? It's only natural."

The wireless officer took a sip of coffee and spat it out in his hand.

"Is there something in it? Hang on, I'll light a match."

"Never mind, don't waste the match. There are no flies or cockcroaches in this heat, and a scorpion wouldn't fit in the cup. I'll tell you about sailors' wives. My mother had an uncle who was a Captain. Fine chap, rich, four ships. In his forties. Married a girl called Zaphirio. Eighteen years old, an orphan, from an upper-class background. Beautiful. He brought master-builders over from Patras and turned the family home into a palace. Mahogany, crystal. Stayed with her for a while, then set off in his best caïque, which he'd named after her. Well he came and he went, and one dawn he set sail for Savona, got back late at night. Put his key in the door, went in and found her under some bloke from Kalamata. Greasy little creep with oiled curls like a queen, who used to travel around Kephallonia selling combs and dress-material and so on.

"Well the guy went to jump out of the window without his trousers, but the Captain caught him from behind by his long curls. Zaphirio didn't make a sound, just hid her face in her hands.

"So the Captain sets the table for three and opens a bottle of Pommery. Caviare, ham, the lot. Forces them to sit down. 'Eat up,' he says, 'you'll need to keep your strength up.' Their adopted child peers in the doorway to see what's going on. 'Off back to bed with you and not a peep, or I'll tan your arse.'

"Well as they were eating and drinking he spilt his wine on the Russian linen tablecloth, and some went on his hand, so he reached over and wet their foreheads. 'Good luck!' he says.

"'Konstanti,' Zaphirio says, 'kill me if you like, but don't torture me. Throw me out in the street, but let me get dressed first.'

"As soon as it was daylight he cut off the legs of the Kalamatan's trousers and threw him out. Had a cup of coffee and went down to the café, where he had his own narghilé. He slept with her that night, and the next. For a month he'd fuck her every night, then set off first thing in the morning to work on his bit of land.

"'Konstanti,' says Zaphirio one lunch-time, 'every day when I make the bed I find you've forgotten some money under the pillow.'

"'I don't forget it. I always pay the whores I sleep with.'

"So it went on, until one lunch-time my great-aunt – as she was – coughed up blood all over the table. She died a few days later. The Captain wouldn't let anyone in the house; he laid her out himself. Then in the middle of the night – they were taking her to the cemetery in the morning – he pulls up her skirts and spits on her thighs. 'Damn you to hell, you bitch.'

"Last time I saw him he was a hundred years old, blind, sitting on a stool in front of the house, facing the sea. That's wives for you."

The First Mate didn't wait before answering: "What kind of a man was that? – Fine fellow! He'd have taken her dowry if she'd had one. But no, she was an orphan and his responsibility. He could have shamed her, he could have killed her, at least been a man about it. By now your great-aunt is a saint, but as for him, better light a candle for him, he'll be wearing a tail where he is now. Not one to flick the flies off, one like the devil's."

The wireless officer tried to light a match. Two, three, four times – the cadet crept up slowly, lighter in hand. "Mister Nikos – I've had a headache since yesterday. And my hair's falling out. D'you suppose it's –"

"Thanks, Diamantis. Nice lighter. Look, we'll see in port. Just don't worry."

The cadet went back to the wheel. For a long time no-one spoke; the only sound was the steady thump of the pistons going up and down. Suddenly the wireless officer started to cough, a dry, irritating cough. He put his handkerchief to his mouth. "Smoker's cough – had it years. The damp ruins the tobacco. Like smoking hay. If we were in Zacharatou now, or a French café, an English pub, we might smell real tobacco. The coffee we drink, dust. The tea's the same. As for the food, better not to talk about it. Drives me crazy when people come aboard in port to eat with the sailors and say how good the ship's bloody macaroni is." He stopped coughing and looked in his pockets for another cigarette.

"Why don't you give it up if it's making you ill?" said Yerasimos.

"It makes *you* ill too; it makes everybody ill. But not one in a thousand gives it up. Listen, if I was on a desert island and I had the choice of a cigarette or a woman, I'd choose the cigarette."

"Rubbish. No-one knows what they'd do when it comes down to it."

"Yes? I was in just that situation once, and I chose the cigarette."

"Actually from what you've been saying I reckon you probably like women rather more than's good for you. Maybe some woman hurt you badly, and that's why you talk the way you do. You'll get over it."

"Balls. Certainly I like them. The sight of a naked woman is a gift of God. But it should be treated as a straightforward business matter. Don't you remember that night in Antwerp? We'd just been paid off from the *Rigel*. Just the two of us, and a dozen girls doing the can-can on the tables. At dawn we worked out the bill. So much for drinks, so much for breakages, and so much for the girls. Six months' pay gone, but I'm pretty sure they weren't giving us the five fingers behind our backs as we left.

"As far as I'm concerned, the real women are the ones you see in iron cages in Tardeo. Or in Yokohama, sitting on stools in shop windows. In the cheap brothels in Foutso, the dirty places in Massawa.

"I remember a bamboo hut, fourteen miles from Colombo. A Senegalese girl, running about naked on all fours, flashing her yellow teeth. Just a rush mat on the earth floor, a jug of water, and a pet bird with funny coloured eyes to catch the mosquitoes. She had some herbs

16

she used to leave smouldering to keep the scorpions away. There I was, lying on my back, worn out with the watches, the damp, the drink, and the body of the girl asleep beside me. I just lay there looking at the bamboo roof. There was a scorpion, dizzy from the smoke, ready to fall right between my eyes. I saw it, but I was so far gone I couldn't move. I just fell asleep.

"I get so sick of those awful words; 'Leave me alone – I don't want to – Tell me you love me first – that you'll never go away.' And when you're done, you can't just get up and leave, no. You've got to console her first, as if you'd beaten her, hurt her. It disgusts me. No, the only good I've ever got from women has been from the ones they call 'Common prostitutes'; they've taught me a thing or two.

"When I was a boy, I used to go to this brothel in Athens, Sakoula's place, in Ghazi. I always went with Arapo, the ugly one from Smyrna. Easy-going, kind. She'd never pass a beggar without giving him something. I was just a kid. She looked after me, used to give me sweets. One night, well past midnight, this driver came and took me off to his place to smoke dope. 'There's a girl there for you, too,' he told me. Arapo just waited for us. She'd probably have washed our feet for us. Well the next morning I left. I was back at Sakoula's place a few days later, looking for Arapo, and when she saw me she ran up, dragging this other girl by the hand: 'Allow me to introduce Kritikia; she's better than me.' I didn't know what to say; threw me completely. 'Yes, Nikoli,' she said, 'It's better like this. You and me used to eat from the same plate. Good luck to you, and whenever you feel like it, bring your friend Michaeli round and we'll eat together.'

"I was best man at her wedding, in a church just outside Athens. She wasn't wearing make-up, and she'd put on a suit made out of an old man's one. She cried right through the service. I saw her once again, during the occupation, hurrying back from the chemist with medicine for her child.

"And another thing: there are places up near the border where when a soldier dies, these women, these 'Common prostitutes', get permission to go in and lay the body out. They sit up with him, and follow the coffin to the church in the morning and wait outside. They even make the burial-offerings."

He stopped to light his cigarette again. "Bloody things keep going out."

"It's the damp," said the First Mate; "everything you touch is wet. Have you done? A whore is a whore. That's their trade, that's their nature. Maybe they have hearts of gold, I wouldn't know. Lots of them get married in the end. As kept women, they're fine. Married, they're useless. There are three trades that need special papers: them, actors and us. The brothel, the boards, and the bridge. Everyone else can change jobs like changing a shirt. Us, never."

Three double bells and a single; a sailor passed them and went down the companionway.

The wireless officer put his hand inside his shirt. "This heat-rash itches. Put on talc and it turns to paste. You were always a blockhead, Yerasimos. Listen, this'll clinch it. I was on the *Poliko*; Piraeus to Saloniki. Now there was a woman – yes, a 'Common prostitute' – just by the hatches, sitting on her trunk. Ugly as a lump of meat. Some deckhand had been hanging around her for ages. 'It's going to be rough, let me find you somewhere to lie down.' 'No.' In the evening he brought her a plate of food. 'I don't want it.' Midnight he was back again. 'Cigarette?' 'No, idiot, can't you see I'm smoking one? Can't you get it into your head I'm not going to come across? I've just left Vourla, and I'm going to Vardari. If you fancy me, come and find me there, but not here. D'you ask the grocer for cheese when you bump into him in the street on Sunday? Go and annoy the first-class passengers and leave me alone.' And at the same time, up in the captain's cabin, there's a high-class respectable lady, four children and a good husband, with her skirt up over her head.

"Have you ever thought what the prostitutes give for their five or ten drachmas? They lie under cripples, blind men, hunchbacks, men who stink of disease, boils all over their bodies, lunatics, all the men who can't find a woman to be good to them. The ones who live in brothels, we call them 'Common prostitutes.' And the others, who live in fine houses, what should we call them, eh? Tell me a name."

The First Mate turned his back and went into the wheelhouse. Dawn. A hot wind blew off the bow. A deckhand and a mechanic came out of the fo'c'sle, buttoning their trousers.

Third Watch

Silent seas, huge but hollow, broke over the foredeck tanks, ran over the hatches and out through the scuppers. The bows of the *Pytheas* would plunge, then she'd lift her head again. She'd been playing this game for twenty-four hours.

Vangelis the bosun, from Pharsa, was talking in his cracked voice to the First Mate. "All in order. Wedges tight. One or two blocks and tackles rolling about, we made them fast. I went aft to check the steering-gear, it's all right. Everything's covered and tied. Listen to it! And it's getting worse."

"O.K. Vangelis, go and rest."

There were flashes of lightning here and there in the east.

"Diamantis!"

The boy came over.

"Go and wake up your uncle. Tell him we're in for bad weather and to come up if he feels like it."

To come up and do what, he thought. To make a nuisance of himself. To piss off the end of the bridge.

Diamantis ran up the companionway, out of breath. "He says he can't come, Captain Yerasimos. He's lying down, he's got a hot water bottle for the pain in his kidneys. He says to do whatever you think best."

The First Mate whistled down to the engine-room and shouted through the voice-pipe. "Cut the revs; half speed."

In a little while the ship sat the waves better. The pitching decreased as if it had suddenly got calmer.

The wireless officer came up and stood a while getting used to the darkness. "Weather report from Hong Kong. Here."

"What does it say?"

"The typhoon's changed course. It's running from Palawan to Mihdoro. I'd say it's a fair way off yet."

"Devil take it," said the First Mate, "that's all we need. With a real ship you'd press on, but with these modern ships you don't want the sea against you. You need distance, keep away from the action. Forty years experience? I've just been lucky. Touch wood. In Biscay six months ago, we'd just passed Ouzan, and the sea got up with the wind.

Four ships went down, two of them new ones. Year before last, in the Black Sea, the weather suddenly turned. North wind, on the beam. Must have felt sorry for us, otherwise we'd never have got through. Then in May of '46, we were just turning for Sydney when a cyclone came up from Tasmania. Either God had pity on us or the devil had forgotten us. But I'm sure we'll find ourselves in the drink one day."

"I came up to get our position," the wireless officer interrupted.

"O.K., Let's go. Didn't you check on the radio D.F.?"

"Yes, but the old system still has its uses."

"Diamantis, stay by the compass, and I'll call back to you."

The boy lifted off the binnacle-hood and put it on the wheelhouse deck. As he bent, the compass-light shone on his face. Unshaven, gaunt, drawn.

The First Mate and the wireless officer went into the chartroom.

"Half a point starboard, but gently."

"Half a point starboard."

"Another half. Bring her up to north-north-east."

"North-north-east it is."

"Keep on that course."

"On course."

"Now, Diamantis, go down and tell your dung-heap of an uncle that we've cut our speed and we're fixing our position. And make us a couple of coffees with a little sugar."

They came out and went to the starboard end of the bridge. The wireless officer got his cigarettes out, but the First Mate stopped him: "Don't light up yet, wait for the coffee. D'you know where the souls of the drowned come out?" He smiled. "From behind. My mother told me that when I first went to sea."

"If they manage to get as far as drowning, Yerasimos. Every sailor's got his own shark waiting for him. And if the shark doesn't get you, something worse will: hospital. Third class. In the corridor, stinking of drains, beds pushed right up against each other. Flies fucking on the faces of the dying. No, I'm afraid of dry land. At least the open sea's clean. And if the fishes eat you, it's natural. We eat them, too."

The First Mate yawned. "Nice subject for a chat. Like a dirge. Can't you find something more cheerful to talk about? If you were married with kids, you'd find a way to get home and die with your family round you. They're not true, the things you say, you don't mean them. You just like saying them. Were you never in love, man?"

He didn't reply at once. First he went over to the wheelhouse window and wrote with his finger on the steamed-up glass. Then he spoke: "The truth's a lie. The biggest, most inhuman lie. You tell the truth to save yourself from the gallows, only then."

"So you never told it?"

"Only once, and I'm still paying for it."

"Was it to save someone's head?"

"No. I nearly lost my own."

"Go on, tell me."

"I was fifteen. At secondary school, the old one. A liar, a whoremonger, and a thief. Every evening I'd go down to Vourla's place. First I'd take a book and sell it, or lift some money from my father's wallet, and get away with it.

"There was a new brothel just opened in Athens then, down near the station. Seventy drachmas. Seven times more than Vourla's or Archontas's, but the girls! There was one from Saloniki I fancied; she'd only just started. It was difficult; I didn't have enough money even for once a week.

"Then I remembered a ring my mother never wore. Gold, with little diamonds. I'd often seen it in her drawer, wrapped up in a bit of paper, separate from her other jewellery. It was easy to steal. We had a day off school, and I went to find my older cousin, who'd know how to shift it. Couldn't find him. I went to a pawnbroker and he chased me out. Tried another and he offered me a hundred drachmas; I told him where to put his hundred drachmas and ran out. 'Never mind,' I thought, 'I'll try again this evening.'

"As I went up the steps of the house I heard Coco, the old parrot, croaking 'Thief! Thief!' It was the only word he knew and I'd heard it a thousand times before, but this time it got to me. I felt pretty bad.

"In the hall I found Meli, a rather tasty maid we had, standing there holding her travelling bag and crying. And there was my mother, furious, saying 'Just tell me the truth.' Well I got the picture. For a moment I was tempted, but I was past the age when young boys are total shits. Actually I had a thing about Meli; I'd often asked her, but she wouldn't. Worse still, she used to tell my mother; I'd been made to feel a fool in front of her. How I hated her. And how beautiful she looked, red-faced and crying.

" 'What's going on?' I said.

" 'Go in and get your dinner,' my mother said.

" 'I'm not going anywhere until you tell me what's going on. What's happened? Maybe I can help.'

"Well she looked at me sideways and said 'A ring's disappeared. I saw it with my own eyes this very morning. No-one's been in my room except her. Now go in and eat.'

"So I put my hand in my waistcoat and pulled the ring out. Held it up between two fingers; 'This the one?'

"Meli's eyes, those lovely weeping eyes, grew big as saucers. My mother's went small and beady; 'Where did you find it?' she said. I'll never forget her voice. Not angry, just despairing.

" 'I didn't find it. I took it, this morning. I stole it, to sell. Here, take it.'

"Off I went down the corridor, and I bumped into my father. He was stroking his beard and smiling. My father – the smuggler of Lao Yan, the card-sharp of Tien Tsin, the grocer from the alleys of Passalimani, the most gutless man I ever knew – my father had forgiven me already. But I still had to square things with my mother."

"And Meli?"

"Meli – well my mother dealt with me out in the wash-room, in front of Meli. She'd brought her in on purpose, to set an example, but then as soon as she'd finished with me she turned on her and cursed her for seeing it all, as if she'd come in of her own accord.

"A few days later, on Sunday, when everyone else was out, Meli came up to me while I was reading. I could feel her breath on me, caressing, burning. She smelt of cheap violets. 'Are you reading?' she said.

" 'Yes.'

" 'Aren't you going out?'

" 'No.'

" 'D'you want me to stay with you?'

" 'No.'

"She started to stroke my head. 'If you like, I'll stay – I'm very grateful for – you know – and if there's anything you want from me –'

" 'Yes, on your way back, pick me up a copy of *Eva* at Yiorgo's stall.'

" 'Nothing else, Mr Niko?'

" 'Nothing.'

"Then she left."

"Did you ever steal again?"

"Oh, yes, lots of times. After we'd gone our separate ways that time in Spain, I went as cadet on a big mailship. They put me in charge of the general goods hold. Middle of the night, New Year's Eve of '30, we were unloading in Piraeus, and the stevedores broke a crate of French clocks. Well we all took one each, then nailed the crate up again properly, with the seals and everything. I tucked mine inside my uniform and went up on deck to go to my cabin. I'd got some boxes of chocolates in my pockets too; I was going to give them to Amersa from Mytilene. I saw the Captain talking to Makrys, the supercargo, and they called me over.

" 'Did you empty number three hold?' Said the supercargo.

" 'Yes, just finished. They're putting the hatches back on now.'

"Then as I was going the Captain called me back. 'Come here a minute,' he said. 'Did you take special care of the crate with the clocks in?'

" 'Oh, yes, Captain Yiorgi.'

" 'Go on, then, off to bed.'

"Well I breathed again, and turned to go. I don't know if the devil was out to get me, or maybe the stevedores were playing a little joke, but just then a bell started ringing inside my uniform. Before they'd worked out what was going on I was up the companionway to the next deck and I ran and hid the damn thing somewhere.

" 'You donkey!' he shouted later, when he kicked my cabin door open, 'You little thief! You'll be lucky to see another day on my ship!' "

Yerasimos laughed.

"You know, I've still got that clock, and it works a treat. How about you, did you ever steal?"

"Oh, I've done my share, rifled the odd hold or two. Once I got into a crate of English shoes. Brown pigskin. I took about a dozen pairs. Called on my mate that night, to share them out. I was quite proud of myself, but he was a real professional. He took one look and shook his head, 'What d'you expect me to do with these, you idiot? They're all right foot!'

"'Find the crate with the left ones?' I said. I tried, but it was hopeless. That shipping agent knew his job. Next trip, same harbour, more crates of shoes. Well we got a few out; all left foot, but black this time. Jewish agent; used to send all his stuff by two or three different lines."

"So what did you do with them?"

"Wait till I tell you. We sold them to some guy in Piraeus who deals in leather goods. Two weeks later he was waiting for us on the quay: 'If you've got any more of those single shoes I'll take them.'

"'What on earth for?' I said.

"'You think I'm crazy, don't you? Well I got in touch with some sort of cripples' self-help organization. Now I'm putting shoes on every one-legged man in the area, and I'm their hero!'

The *Pytheas* rolled gently on a quiet sea; somewhere the weather had spent its force. Captain Yerasimos went into the wheelhouse, turned on the light and came out again. He leant on the rail by the wireless officer, lit a cigarette and started to talk again: "I asked you before. Were you never in love?"

"No. Not as far as I can remember. I was in too much of a hurry, always with a suitcase in my hand. Used to keep a full kit-bag just inside the door of the house. What about you?"

"Me? It happened once. Still burns. We were tied up for four months in Saigon. After the first few days everyone found somewhere on shore, there were only a few of us left on board. Some Chinaman wanted to sell me a girl, they used to do that in those days. He took me off to some slum, stank of garlic and rotten eggs. Well there was a sort of landlord there, with seven girls, not to mention the boys. 'Take your pick,' he told me. 'Don't be shy if you prefer a boy, but I'd advise you to take that girl there,' and he pointed at a skinny, dirty little creature of about thirteen. 'Don't be put off,' he said, 'In a couple of days she'll look fine. Tao! Come here!'

"The little girl came up, staring at the floor.

"'Take her,' the guy who'd brought me said; 'She just needs fattening up.'

"So I paid fifteen dollars and off we went. I took her to a shop and told them to give her a good wash and dress her. Well an hour later you wouldn't have known her; her face was shining. As we went to the ship she was clinging to my jacket, running to keep up. I took her into a cake shop. She ate great handfuls of cake, and laughed. It was night already; we stopped at a little roadside stall and I bought her a coral bracelet, but she wouldn't have it; she chose a ball and a spinning-top.

"As we went up the gangplank Captain Yanni from Spartia – God rest his soul – caught my eye, and he gave me the five fingers with both hands. 'Dirty sods, turning my ship into a kindergarten. I'll make you pay every day for their food. The chief mechanic says we've used up five gallons of paraffin getting the lice off them. Dirty sods.'

"When we got to my bunk I could tell it was the first time she'd been with a man. She brought one hand up and covered her face. She ground her teeth – I don't know if they all do that the first time – and with the other hand she kept fiddling nervously with the cross I wore round my neck.

"'Why are you crying, Tao?' I asked, in broken English.

"'No— No sorr— Go on— Please put on the light.'

"She was up before dawn. She made me tea, polished my shoes, then she set about tidying the cabin. She didn't know one end of a ship from the other, but she'd learnt to cook. And can you believe it, that great bear Captain Yanni used to bring her sweets and toffee-apples. All the other girls on board – a lazy, stinking lot – had a very easy time, lying around all day in their men's cabins, or in the fo'c'sle.

"Finally we had to set sail for Bordeaux. Suddenly all the other girls were gathering up their things and going down the gangplank with long faces. I'd explained to her the evening before, as gently as I could. She didn't stop crying all night. I had every right to take her with me, she said; after all I'd paid for her. Of course the Captain wouldn't hear of it, and anyway, where could I take her? My people in Kephallonia wouldn't have stood for it. In the end I went to talk to the Chinaman who'd found her for me.

"'Is that all that's worrying you?' he said, grinning. 'Sell her to some brothel and get your money back.' Well of course I wasn't going to do that. 'In that case, take her back where you got her— better still, just leave her on the quay to sort it out for herself.'

"That afternoon I told her to get dressed. She put her European clothes on; a green suit, high-heeled shoes. Off we went. The sweat was running down her forehead, and she was grinding her teeth again, just like that first night. When the rickshaw stopped outside the place where I'd bought her, she suddenly took my hand and squeezed it as tight as she could— we went up to the door, and she looked around at the dirty alley-way. When the old landlord came he gave us a black look. We tore up our agreement, and I watched her fiddling nervously with the bits of paper. I wanted to get away, but it was as if I had lead shoes on. Tao fell on her knees and clung to my jacket— All I could hear, as I turned the corner of the alley, was a wailing sound, like the wind splitting a canvas awning.

"It was about two miles to the harbour; I started to run. There in Catinat Street, right by the stall where I'd bought her the bracelet but she'd chosen the toys instead, I stopped to get my breath. I leant panting and sweating against a pillar; a couple of coolies saw me and screamed 'Cholera, cholera!' and ran off.

"We weighed anchor the next day. I've been back to Saigon many times since. The guy who arranged the deal's dead now. They've knocked down the slum where she lived; it's a park and French schools now. Bordellos, cabarets, casinos, opium dens, all gone. Nothing left. But sometimes at night, I swear I can hear her crying."

"You got off easily. Come on, let's check the course."

The engine-room speaking-tube whistled. "Yes. Keep the same engine speed. If it's calmed down by morning, we'll open her up a bit." He closed the pipe and turned. "Where's Diamantis? He's been gone an hour, the little sod. And who's at the wheel?" He opened the pipe again and blew the whistle.

The wireless officer breathed on the wheelhouse window and wrote with his finger.

Diamantis crept quietly up the starboard companionway; the other cadet came up the port side and went to the wheel. The First Mate had calmed down; "Where've you two been?" Nobody answered him.

The wireless officer called Diamantis over; they talked quietly.

"Are you sure?"

"Yes."

"Since when?"

"I first noticed it yesterday."

"Why didn't you come and tell me?"

"I did— yesterday."

"Come to my cabin as soon as the watch changes."

The First Mate had overheard; "I'll come too. Got anything to drink?"

"We'll find something. I'll expect you, then."

Yerasimos stood silently, looking ahead. Then he went over and breathed on the wheelhouse window. He looked carefully. "The cuckold," he murmured, "The son of a whore." He wiped the glass with his sleeve and turned to the helmsman. "Steer to starboard. Bear down on the green light."

The wireless-operator's cabin. Low-ceilinged, long and narrow. An unmade bunk. A dirty wash-basin, under it a bucket full of turbid water. A table against the bulkhead, loaded with books, scraps of paper, boxes of matches, an old wallet, a Chinese tobacco-pouch and scattered cigarettes. A saucer full of butts. On the bunk, on the floor, on the chair, more scattered cigarettes. The glass shelf above the wash-basin full of medicines: Opobyl, Carlsbad salts, fruit salts and iodine. On a line stretched from one corner to the other hung a badly-washed pair of underpants, a vest and a pair of socks. On the floor an open carton of Craven A. In a corner a crate half-full of apples and oranges gave off a faint smell of mould. The walls covered with coloured pictures cut from *Life*.

The wireless-operator, naked to the waist, was putting talc on his spotty shoulders and chest. Captain Yerasimos appeared in the doorway.

"Sit down, I'm just finishing."

"Is there somewhere to sit? You're swimming in filth. How often does the steward come to clean?"

"The sod always comes when I'm sleeping. Never mind, so much the better. Whenever he tidies he upsets the order of my cabin. I used to quarrel with my mother whenever she moved a book or a paper – have a cigarette. Can I peel you an apple?"

"No."

"I could clean you some pineapple –"

"In the bucket you wash your feet in, or with water from that bottle that wouldn't come clean if you used caustic soda? I'll have a cigarette. What is it with you and cigarettes? Scattered wherever you look. And yet I've often noticed you have plenty of full packets. D'you steal them, or does someone give you them? I can't understand the waste. Why d'you do it?"

The wireless-operator tossed the talc onto a shelf and sat down on a stool. The mate had lain down on the bunk, the pillow doubled behind his head.

"The things you ask! If anyone else asked I'd say 'Because I feel like it.' You know how it is with cigarettes. When you haven't got any – when –"

"I've known that in prison."

"It's even worse out. In Albania once, I'd lost my company for two days. Soaking wet, starving, and no cigarettes. Dawn; a beautiful day. Feast of St Nicholas. The sun playing on the wet greenery. I was walking along, leading a hungry mule. Suddenly I saw a soldier standing in my way.

"'What happened to you?' he said.

"'What d'you think? You haven't come across the Third Medical Corps by any chance?'

"'Yes. They've set up camp three hours' journey on, in Pepeli monastery. Straight ahead as you're going.'

"I made to leave.

"'Wait,' he said. He opened his bag and cut me a lump of army bread. He turned to go, then came back. He opened a red packet of Number Ten and gave me a cigarette. I took it in my hand and stared at it. He put another one into my hand and went off quickly.

"'What's your name?' I called; 'Wait – what's your name?'

"'My name's "Soldier",' he shouted through his cupped palms, 'Hurry up before it gets dark, or they'll be gone.'

"I watched him until he was out of sight. I put the bread in my bag and lay down under a tree. Lit the cigarette—

—"Come in then, Diamantis. All right, bend your head down. Bit more."

Under the boy's blond hair, which was thinning, there was white scurf.

"It's the sea that's making your hair fall out, Diamantis. Haven't you heard of that? All's well. I can't see anything you need to worry about. How's the abscess?"

"The same. It bleeds now and then."

"That means it's getting better. You know where we're travelling. It's a bad climate; you expected better? You'll forget your worries in port. We'll go to the doctor's together, then you'll buy us a drink. Go and sleep now, and if you see a girl in your dreams, chase her away, so you'll be in good condition where we're going."

"And the headache?" asked the boy as he was getting dressed.

"We've all got one. Off you go."

They listened to his footsteps fading across the deck.

"He's won the big medal – I told you from the start. And it's getting worse. Have you got any penicillin?"

"Yes."

He scratched his head nervously; "But we shouldn't give him anything. I've got a course of bismuth, but it's not on. If he hasn't got it? Am I a doctor? We'll find out when he has the first injection. It's confusing, you see. But that abscess. 'Di Castel,' they call it. It's a sure sign. How frightened he is! Well, I was scared the first time. Thought my nose would drop off."

"And I thought I'd go blind. Don't take any notice when I treat him roughly, I love the little sod. He's got good reason to be afraid; d'you remember his father?"

"No. I heard something."

"He went mad, up on the bridge. The boy would have heard about it; how not to, in villages like ours? People do you the kindness of letting you know; such a favour. D'you love Kephallonia?"

"Yes, as a place. But we're cruel to cripples and madmen; that's something I can't take."

"Oh, rubbish. They're like that in every village in the world."

"No, in my place they drive people mad deliberately, to have someone to laugh at."

"You're exaggerating. You're more stubborn than a mule. What were we saying about cigarettes?" He yawned and rubbed his eyes.

"Leave it for tomorrow, so we'll have something to talk about. Time to sleep for a few hours."

The mate got up, brushing the ashes from his trousers: "I'm going up to take a look. You know, sometimes the old man loses himself up on the bridge."

"It gets to him?"

"Not exactly. How to put it – he freezes."

"Poor chap. How old is he?"

"Sixty-five and then some. How the wheel rolls! First officer for years. And a sailor – for ever."

"Good morning. I'm going to copy the dead." He pulled the faded red curtain across the porthole.

Fourth Watch

> *May Buenos Aires burn and Cardiff flood,*
> *But God protect my poor old Skipper Straad.*

It had been raining since morning.

The First Mate was on watch outside the wheelhouse, wearing oilskins. From time to time he got his binoculars out, but soon put them away again.

"Look-out—"

"It's me, Captain Yerasimos, Polychronis."

"Go down and turn the lights out in the saloon. Then go forward and find the wireless officer and ask him to come up if he isn't doing anything. Don't be long."

"All right, Captain Yerasimos, I'm on my way."

"Diamantis, check to port and starboard and then keep a good look-out ahead. If you need to go for a pee, come and tell me. Why aren't you wearing oilskins?"

"I feel hot."

The First Mate lifted the window and wiped it inside and out. He took off his oilskins and hung them on a nail, then stood gazing ahead. He remembered the rains in his village. Two, three, four days— the time of year when they'd be taking the goatskins off the cheese and opening the new oil. The vine, that stank of barrel-staves— it was an hour to school, on foot. He stayed at home and looked at the copy of *Robinson Crusoe* with its torn pages. He could smell the food cooking. They were waiting for letters and money from Argentina, Canada, Marseilles. On just such a day the message had come that his father had been drowned off Kavakia. At sixteen years old he'd set off one morning, in the rain, for his first voyage—

"It's unhealthy, this rain," he muttered.

Polychronis came up, making a lot of noise: "I didn't turn the lights out because the Captain was reading, but I closed the curtains. He said I could turn them off if they were a nuisance. The wireless officer's a bit strange – humming to himself – what can I say – weird noises. I think he'll go crazy, like that other one before. I listened to him raving for a long time. He picks up a book, opens it, and throws it down. And those nudes he's got on the walls of that stable of a cabin – completely mad. We'll lose him over the stern-rail, sure as I'm standing here."

"Did you tell him to come?"

"No, as soon as I turned up he waved me away. Is he one of our people?"

"Yes, from Erissos. But he was born where we're going now."

"What? Chinese parents?"

"No, idiot; Kephallonians."

"Have you seen how he goes about? There's not a single button on his flies. And they say he was on the passenger ships for years; did he go about like that there too?" He turned round and saw the wireless officer beside him. "Oh Lord— I came to get you, but you were talking."

"Go and make us a couple of coffees," said the First Mate. "Take the good coffee from my cabin, and don't put too much sugar in."

"Can I make one for myself?"

"Go ahead, boy, but the stuff you drink's like syrup. What time have you got?" he asked, turning to the wireless officer.

"Five past two. At midnight, just as I was getting ready to come up, the old man came to the wireless cabin. 'Can you get Piraeus?' he says. 'I can try.' 'London?' 'Bit better.' He gave me a couple of telegrams for the office. He writes worse than a Catholic from Chios; I've only just finished now. Atmospherics, interference, nothing else. And sparks on the aerial. Had to happen now! My head's ringing like a bell. What was Polychronis telling you?"

"What would he be telling me, the clown? He's just an ox from Kalliakra. Completely stupid. When he was twelve he was cabin-boy on a caïque and he fell from the mast. And when his wife left him, three days after the wedding, it finished him. And he's still young; thirty. Why did they give her to him? Beautiful, and she'd been to school in Argostoli. He came back after the occupation loaded with money, food and clothes. Her people were hungry, they gave her to him. The strange thing is, she was willing! Talk about women— wasn't a week before she was back home."

"Didn't say why?"

"No idea— it's a long story."

"Oh, come on, he must have let something slip sometime."

"They still talk about it— Shh, he's coming."

Polychronis came up, pulling up the tray with two cups and the coffee-pot on a long wire behind him. He put the cups on the parapet and filled them.

"And yours?" the First Mate asked.

"I'll drink mine from the pot."

"How many cockcroaches in each cup?"

"They fell in too quickly to count." He drank, making slurping noises.

"Tell me, Polychronis," the wireless officer asked suddenly, "why aren't you married?"

Polychronis stopped with the coffee-pot at his lips. He tried to make out the wireless officer's eyes in the darkness. Then he slurped up the dregs and answered. "Well, I was once. But it was no good; we separated."

"Marry again. Are there no more women?"

Yerasimos nudged him with his elbow, but he moved away a little and carried on: "You should have children, leave the sea."

"Mister Nikos, I'm scared of women. Women and hatchways. You can slip on either and wreck yourself. Twice is too often."

"How did you separate? Just like that, for no reason?"

"Oh— how can I say— who knows what went on in her mind, those three nights?"

"Maybe, that first night—"

The First Mate cleared his throat; "Listen, Polychronis—"

"Please, Captain Yerasimos. I'm going. But look, it's not my fault – our countryman here asked."

"Let him carry on, Yerasimos, he's got nothing important to do. We know more; maybe we can work it out."

"If the cap fits— did I say anything? I'm going blind keeping a look-out ahead, I didn't even hear what you were saying, don't blame me," and he moved away a little.

Half unwillingly, Polychronis drew close to the wireless officer and started to talk, quickly and confusedly, now and then glancing over at the First Mate. "Look, Mister Niko, now we've started I'll tell you the whole thing from the beginning. I swear to you, I've never even told my mother, and she crucified me to get it out of me. Nor my father. But never breathe a word of it, because there are some rotten bastards around."

"We're not children, Polychronis. If you're afraid, don't tell me."

"Well, after we'd eaten, and drunk a drop of wine, my mother took me aside and said 'I'm telling you for your own good, don't be rough with her. Gently does it.'

"We went to our house, and when we were in the bedroom and we'd sat on the bed, I got up and locked the door, and put the key on the table. She gets up suddenly and says 'Unlock it, Polychronis, because I'm up and going right this minute.'

" 'But— Why?'

" 'I'm afraid, I tell you. Unlock it.'

" 'Afraid of me, Marioleni?'

" 'I don't know. Unlock it, and put the light out.'

"I did as she said. Ever since I was a young lad, ever since I first went to Vourla's place, wherever I went, whenever I was with a woman I used to keep the door locked and the lamp lit.

"Anyway to cut a long story short, nothing— first time that had happened to me. I could just make out her face in the dawn light. Colour of Katania sulphur. Then suddenly, I don't know how, she accidentally put the sole of her foot—"

"Polychronis, the log!" Shouted Captain Yerasimos.

"Just a minute, let me finish, Captain Mema, then I'll go."

"Sod you. The log. Fuck your pride."

Polychronis ran down the companionway. For five minutes, only the thump-thump of the engine and the splash of water on the ship's sides could be heard.

"Seventy-five and a half."

"O.K," the First Mate answered quietly.

"Well—" Polychronis continued.

"Polychronis, go down to my cabin and bring me the red book with the anchor on it. Take a swig or two of rum and then come and take over the wheel, so Dionysis can go for a pee."

"Oh, he doesn't need one. I asked him and he doesn't want to go."

"Do as I say, or –"

Polychronis hesitated, then left, turning his head once or twice to mutter "To hell with him. The mule can kick him with all four hooves, the first time –"

The rain had stopped some time before; there was only lightning. Nikos was sitting on the locker where the lifebuoys were kept. He was remembering the afternoon in Bordeaux, when he'd gone with the cigarette-girl in the Oceania Bar. She'd been in a hurry and left the counter unattended. The red woollen shawl around her shoulders – a room just behind the counter – "Gauloises bleues s'il vous plait –" She'd got up and left him. Since then he couldn't smoke French cigarettes, not Gitanes, not –

Yerasimos had his back turned, looking ahead – and into himself – the *San Paoli* – the blonde girl who – who wasn't any – he wiped away the sweat with his damp handkerchief – sex.

The wireless officer's hand rested gently on his shoulder. "Come back here, Yerasimos. Have a cigarette."

"Just a moment – wait."

"What's up? Shall I go?"

"No, stay. Wait for that idiot to come back, so you can lance his boil. I've been admiring your skill all this time."

"Don't kid yourself. I've been scraping at my own boil with Polychronis's lance."

"You don't need to scratch your wounds, they hurt by themselves. You're a deep one."

"You think I was asking out of curiosity, or to make fun of him?"

"We're all tickled by things like that, only we don't admit it. And how you can fish it out of him! Without bait; you're an expert."

"You're wrong. Anyone could have asked him just at that moment, and he'd have told."

"Yes – lots have asked. You picked the moment."

"Tell me, did Marioleni marry again?"

"No."

"Did they get divorced?"

"I haven't asked him."

"I'm sure if Marioleni took another man, he'd leave her within a week, for the same reason she left Polychronis."

"Fairy tales. The heat's turned your brain."

"Well, I'm going to make him sit down and write her a letter."

"He doesn't know how to write."

"I'll write it for him. I'll bet you fifty rupees she'll send him a telegram, 'I'm waiting for you.'"

"The ideas that get into your head! Kephallonian girls never change their minds."

"Kephallonian girls, Chios girls – they're all women. Have a cigarette."

"I've just put one out. You waste them, you leave half."

"Have you smoked dog-ends? Other people's leavings? It's misery. I'll tell you something, and don't laugh.' He bent to whisper in the First Mate's ear. "Sometimes, at night, I throw a full packet in the sea. It's an offering."

"For the unknown soldier?"

"And the unknown woman. One particular woman – the time when the fares were low, the big crisis – but I'm boring you, I'll go."

"Oh, come on, you want me to beg you? Out with it."

"I was in Antwerp, without a ship. I got through the first month, but then a hard winter set in. I got a couple of weeks heavy work on a ship from Chios. Working up in the rigging, nearly froze to death, but I had hopes they'd take me with them. They tricked me; I was left on the dock watching them set sail for Argentina. I used to eat in that restaurant run by one of our people, you remember him? Well, one day I didn't have the money to pay. 'Chalk it up,' I told him, 'and as soon as I get a ship I'll pay you back.'

" 'I know you would,' he said, 'but it's not up to me. Gladys looks after the books.' Gladys was his wife. A smelly hippopotamus; she used to beat him up too.

"So I started to sell things. My gold watch, the buttons off my shirt. I ran out of things to sell. Just when things got really tight I met a chap from Ithaca, a card-sharp. 'Want to help me cut up the bread?' he said. What could I do? I agreed. Didn't take him long to teach me. We'd go to good places, well-run. Me at one table, him at another. Greek tobacco-dealers, shipping agents, students, would come in and say 'We're looking for a fourth; d'you play cards, my friend?'

" 'A bit.'

" 'Just for small change. Come and join us.'

"I'd pretend not to want to.

" 'Just to pass the time.'

"We had the clothes off their backs without their realizing it. Pile of money. He cheated me on the share-out, but what could I do? Then I found a hotel, on Skipper Straad, where else? Among the brothels, the cafés and the cheap cabarets. A tiny attic room. Cheap. I could only go there after eight in the evening. At seven in the morning they'd ring a bell right over your head, it didn't stop till you'd gone, the whole hotel was ringing. By ten past seven you had to be out, and then another lot of people would start coming up the stairs. You see? It was the night workers: waiters, night-watchmen, cabaret girls, whores. You'd see them as you went out – coal-blackened faces, frozen faces, faces whose make-up had got smeared onto other people's cheeks, faces wrinkled and eaten by the salt spray, all going to lay themselves down in our beds, warm and unmade, just as we'd left them.

"From the first night I realized I was sharing my bed with a girl of the night. A pair of stockings hanging on a nail, a worn-out pair of slippers trimmed with black bows, a pair of knickers under the pillow, scattered hairpins, broken combs decorated with fake jewels. But above all, the scent of her body. I'd rest my head on a pillow that was always dented by her head, marked by her hair-oil – she must have had long black hair. I wanted to get to know her, but I knew it was out of the question. It was an old rule of the place that the night tenant should never know the day one. I started to go about looking for her –"

Yerasimos interrupted him with a cough: "If you didn't know her, how could you find her? Like a needle in a haystack – you could walk right by her, you could talk to her, without realizing."

"Impossible. I didn't find her anywhere, but if she'd come within ten metres of me, I'd have known her."

"How the devil – ?"

"Listen. I've learnt two skills in life. One – I've lost it now – I could tell from the way a drunk staggered what had made him drunk. Or from his breath. Or you could mix as many different drinks as you liked in one glass and I could tell you them one by one. I can't do it since I stopped drinking. The other's with me still, and I won't lose it till I die." He stopped a moment.

"Well?"

"Blindfold me, or put me in a dark room at night. Get half-a-dozen women, or a dozen, or a hundred, as many as you like, to walk past me, and I can tell you the nationality of each one."

"Oh, and how old they are too, I suppose – have you seen a doctor lately?"

"Just from the scent of their bodies, the air around them."

"Finish the Antwerp story."

"Well around that time I had a final bust-up with the chap from Ithaca. I settled accounts, then started to make economies. Cut my cigarettes in half, lived off bread and cheese. I wanted to spend the winter under a roof, not under a bridge. One night, as I was going off to bed without a cigarette in my pocket, I found an ashtray full of dog-ends stained with fire-red lipstick. 'They're only going to be thrown out,' I thought. I peeled off the paper and put the tobacco in my pipe. Another time I found two or three cigarettes on the table, a bit tatty but still in one piece – as if someone had been playing with them nervously, or they'd been loose in someone's pocket. I looked at them for a long time, but I hadn't the nerve to take them. I've never suffered worse torture. As soon as I woke up I reached for them, but 'There'll be trouble,' I thought, and I left, running. The next evening I found them still in the same place, and a bit of paper by them: 'Can to smoke – for you –' it said, in crooked handwriting. From then on I found something every night. A sandwich, a half-eaten apple, a bottle with a few dregs, and cigarettes. My socks washed and darned, my handkerchiefs ironed. It seemed someone felt for me; was trying to help.

"In February – that terrible winter – the *Argonaut* came in to unload minerals. My uncle was the Captain. He saw the state I was in. 'I'll take you,' he said, 'but sort yourself out.'

"I started eating better. I told him I was drowning in debts and I had to pay them off, and he gave me a sub. So I went to the biggest florist in Antwerp, somewhere in the Longue Rue des Images, and bought the most expensive flowers I could find. Dahlias. Then I bought a big box of chocolates and set off for Skipper Straad. I'd go to my room – our room – I'd put them on the table, where I'd found the cigarettes. No, the flowers on the dirty pillow – I felt a bit of a fool carrying them. A hundred yards before I got there, this fat woman with a cigarette in her mouth and an artificial flower in her hair came out of an alley and stopped me.

" 'You getting engaged then, Bob?' she asked me, laughing.

" 'Out of my way,' I said, pushing her gently.

" 'Come and buy me a drink.'

" 'Later; I'm in a hurry now.'

" 'Just a few minutes, then you can go, I won't keep you.'

"I refused again, but she pushed me into this dirty little place – just one – then another – and another – plenty of time, it was still daylight –

"I can't remember how many. I can remember the police pulling me out of the gutter at dawn. Some trampled flowers beside me. Someone had stolen the chocolates. At midday we left for Hull – did you say something?"

"No – yes: what perfume did she wear, that woman?"

"The one in the bar?"

"No, the one in the hotel."

"*Styx*, by Coty."

"Where could the seagulls find to shit you out?" muttered the First Mate. "You ought to be shot. With a pistol full of shit."

Fifth Watch

The Third Officer – twenty-four years old, tall, fine dark features – turned on the wheelhouse light, took out a folded piece of paper and unwrapped a photograph. He showed it to the helmsman.

Linatseros held it up, screwing up his eyes to look. Suddenly the light went out. "Beautiful. But if that's the way she wants it – don't let it kill you. There's plenty more women – I wish I were your age."

The Third Officer took the photograph back and tried to look at it in the darkness.

"Why don't you throw it away, Captain Pantelis? She can go and look for your first pair of shoes, and you can forget her."

"Is it that easy, Linatseros? Just think, I got the wedding-rings in Colombo. Gold was cheap. Got her a tourmaline too; pink and green. Beautiful. I go back to the ship, and get the letter the same day."

"And is he good-looking, the other guy? Young?"

"Yes. Just out of college. Midshipman."

"Ah – I see. Our ranks aren't good enough, they're just for fun. Captain Pantelis, it's better like this. I know what I'm talking about. I wish mine had left me before the wedding, I'd have been a different man now."

"I heard rumours. Did you separate?"

"Did we separate! I was smuggling for her sake. I fixed up the little house in Tabouria like a palace. What didn't I do for her, what else could she want?— I gave up the mailships and worked on freighters. Her letters— dripping with honey. I was away two years. We got back to Piraeus one winter's night; it was late before we'd got finished. Midnight had struck by the time I set off, loaded with stuff, for home. On the corner before the house I stopped to change hands because my kit was heavy. Outside my house some guy was throwing pebbles at the window. Had I got the wrong house? What does that cuckold want, at this hour? Suddenly he grabbed the two handles and kicked the door, shouting 'Come out you worthless whore, and bring out that creep you've got with you so I can tear him apart.'

"I came closer; 'My friend,' I said, 'What's the matter?'

"'Mind your own business,' he said, without turning round.

"I grabbed him by the shoulder; 'What's going on, eh?'

"He turned round angrily. 'Bugger off, if you know what's good for you. I've got business with the lady of the house.'

"'Fine, but why are you taking it out on the doors and windows?'

"'I'll smash everything, your head too, if you don't keep out of my affairs.'

"'I see,' I said, calmly. 'But what you're smashing here, I built myself, by keeping long watches on the bridge. D'you understand?'

"His face fell and he stepped back, murmuring 'How was I to know?' and then he disappeared round the corner.

"I put my kit-bag and suitcase down, sat down nearby and waited. There was no other door. Two o'clock struck. I heard the door opening: I turned and watched someone come out; chap with a fat gut and a face like a hawk. Never even noticed me. I waited five minutes and put my key in the door.

"'Who's there?'

"'Me, Stamatis.'

"She gave a yell and fell into my arms. 'Oh, my man, my big boss, I've been so miserable longing for you.'

"She pulled me towards the bedroom, but I dragged her into the dining-room. Full of stale tobacco-smoke, enough to choke you. Two plates with left-overs, a bottle of wine.

"'Don't tell me you've taken up smoking?' I said.

"'No, it was our best man— he came by earlier to ask after you and stayed to dinner. He left, oh, about nine.'

"'And this, eh, what's this?' and I pointed at a cigarette that had fallen out of the ashtray and was burning the tablecloth.

"'Come on, you poor old thing— Just arrived and already you're moaning. I had one myself because I couldn't sleep— I've missed you—' and she started to cry.

"'And that creep who was beating on the door at midnight, calling you filthy words so everyone could hear, I suppose that was your godfather?'

"She turned pale. 'I don't understand you. Are you drunk, or has the voyage turned your mind? Come on, sit down and I'll make you a cup of tea.'

"I held my hand up to stop her. 'Just a word or two. You can have it all. The house and everything— no discussion, no fuss. Go to the lawyer tomorrow and make the papers. Me, I went to the brothels in every port, so we're quits. Bye.'

"She stood there like a marble statue. 'Let me do your washing for you; I'll bring it to you tomorrow.'

"'Don't bother; you'll only get a bad back with all the bending.'

"I gathered up my things and went and knocked on the door of an Armenian girl I'd known before I was married. She took me in without a word."

"And what became of your wife?" asked the third officer in a broken voice.

Linatseros reached up to the bell over his head and gave a double ring. "Oh— I never saw her again. I found out later that some bloke had taken her for everything she'd got— up in Vourla."

"Horrible. Weren't you sorry? Didn't you suffer?"

"What sort of talk's that? Suffer— Stranger's flesh doesn't count. I'd suffer for my mother— D'you remember the other wireless officer? Ha! Two days before we got to Piraeus, all the married guys sent telegrams to their wives. The wireless officer came out and stood on top of the main bunker, shouting 'Anyone else for a telegram? Come on, so the lover-boys will have time to get away.' And we thought he was crazy."

The third officer went out of the wheelhouse, breathing hard. He took out his handkerchief. He stood at the rail a long time, trying to make out the sea in the darkness. Four bells rang. Change of watch.

"Wind North-North-East, sea clear to starboard."

"Clear to starboard," the First Mate acknowledged. The look-out brought him his coffee and put it on top of the lamp-housing; "I've left it there, don't knock it over."

"Fine," answered the First Mate.

Diamantis was wearing a big blue coat with a thick collar.

"Hey, boy, didn't you bring a crow-bar too, so we can chip off the ice? What's the idea? Or maybe you're taking the same treatment as your uncle? You'll roast."

"What treatment, Captain Yerasimos?"

"Oh— nothing. Come on, I'll teach you something. Can you see Venus? Looks good tonight. Let's wait for her to rise a bit." He took a sip or two of coffee. "Bring me the sextant, Diamantis. Don't put the light on. Yes, give it to me— you check the chronometer."

"Ready."

He brought the star to the horizon— "Now. Check the log."

The star looked like one eye of a satiated whore. Her lover had poked out the other with his finger.

"What are you looking at?" asked the wireless officer, who was standing a little way off.

"Oh, I'm looking for the Southern Cross. I used to be able to find it on my own."

"It's set now. The other watch must have seen it for a while. Don't you see, we've come north, and the further we go— how can you forget? Well, you were never too bright. Remember the time you ran up the quarantine flag?"

"D'you ever bring yours down?"

"No. I could never manage it. You seem to have a thing about the Southern Cross."

"Yes. You've never felt its fever, its heaviness."

"What are you talking about? Is it malaria, or am I supposed to carry it, like a porter? All the stars are beautiful. They're useful to us when we can find them so many degrees above the horizon, otherwise they're for loving couples in the parks to count. Go up early, on the eight to twelve, to be in time to see it— There was a girl once, who loved the Southern Cross—"

"And you loved the girl."

"No."

"Was she beautiful?"

"I never knew her. And she never knew the sea, never saw the Southern Cross—"

"You keep saying 'Never' tonight. Have you got a photo of her?"

"No. But she used to write to me— such letters!"

"Have you still got them?"

"No. I threw them all in the sea, in Shark Bay. Listen. I promised to take her on a voyage. Not the way we promise all the women we meet, because I didn't know her. In those days I was in the Med.; 1937. I fixed it up with the office to take her on a round trip, and sent her a letter. But then we couldn't leave Piraeus; waiting for coal. I hung about for ages on the jetty. Just think, to let her down over something she'd longed for, to make a fool of her, however unwillingly. I never wrote to her again after that."

"You'd told so many lies, one more couldn't hurt."

"I never lied, I'd arranged it all, I tell you, just as I would for my own sister."

"Never mind," said Yerasimos sarcastically, "She was lucky. You'd have screwed it up one way or another, I know you of old. They're all your sisters, then in the end you get them by the arse. Do me a favour. Poor sod."

"You're in a bad mood tonight. Didn't you get your coffee? You've been getting at me ever since I came up. I'm going to bed."

"Come on, I was joking. What became of the girl?"

"Oh— I think she got married."

"Shame she didn't wait for you. Did you never try to find her, get to know her?"

"No. Sometimes I think of her, just before I go to sleep. Some time, some night, without telling her, I'll go to Volos and knock on her door. Take her on a trip. I could do it, now."

"And afterwards?"

"Afterwards? I hadn't thought further than that."

The First Mate turned round quickly and grabbed him by the shoulder: "Afterwards," he said heavily, weighing his words, "Afterwards – and there's always an afterwards for you, my Chinese river-boy – afterwards you'd have sold her in the Beirut bordellos for two hundred souris, like the Mytilene girl." Suddenly he regretted what he'd said; his voice softened: "Forget that. They told me something, but I didn't believe it. I meant to ask you. Forgive me." The First Mate loosened his grip on the wireless officer's shoulder, but left his hand there, like a caress. The wireless officer, without a word, made as if to go, but he held him back. "If you go now, I'll think I've offended you."

"Let me go."

"Out of the question. It's my fault— I swear it on my mother's honour, and I've never done that before: I didn't mean to upset you. I didn't believe it, but I wanted to ask you how the story got about. I was too blunt – we're sailors, not diplomats. Fancy a coffee?"

"Got any cognac?"

"Yes, but you don't drink."

"Just a drop."

"Polychronis, fetch the bottle and two raki glasses." He went into the wheelhouse and bent over the compass a moment.

Polychronis filled the glasses, then licked his fingers. "Something tells me you've been at that bottle," said the First Mate.

"May I lose my mind! May I be delivered bound into the hands of the saints! But I was thinking of asking you to offer me one."

"You're still on duty. When the watch changes."

"Cheers. Safe harbour." The wireless officer lifted his glass and smelt the drink. "It's been three years – is this French?"

"Yes, Armagnac."

He drank it drop by drop, like medicine. "D'you think it'll make me ill?"

"Don't know. Better not drink any more."

"Well. You want to know the truth of it?"

"No. I'm not curious. I was going to talk about something else."

"You wanted us to quarrel again."

"Never again, touch wood. Something came over me. Wrong moment."

"I had a monkey once, a crafty little biter. Worthless. I took her through the customs in Piraeus, had to pay a pile of money. As I was going to get on the tram some gypsy stopped me: 'A thousand francs, effendi.' I didn't understand what he wanted. 'Two thousand.' I understood. 'Leave me alone,' I told him. By the time we got to the station it was ten thousand. I'd come back to Greece penniless; ten thousand was a fortune in those days. I took the bait and gave her away. I'm still ashamed of it all these years later. No—"

The First Mate went back into the wheelhouse and called down to the engine-room. "We're hardly moving tonight," he said when he came back. "Might as well be at anchor. It's the Algerian and the Syrian in the stokehold this watch. They laze about every evening, but tonight there's no steam at all. One or two shovels full, then they lie down. Never do any raking-out. What the devil— he smokes something, the black dog. This afternoon I turned his bunk and locker upside down, but all I could find was caporal and papers. So I spoke to the Syrian; he was all 'I don't know anything, my Captain.' They're in it together, I reckon."

"Hashish?"

"Can't work it out. What's that other stuff called, what the devil is it?"

"Marijuana?"

"Yes."

"It's dried roots."

"How's it smoked?"

"There's a special way. But it'll burn in a pipe."

"Does it stink?"

"Ooh! The whole neighbourhood and forty more."

"That first engineer, he couldn't give a damn. 'Don't worry,' he says to me this morning, 'We're still moving – what's your hurry?' What could I say? He's like an army mule, the cuckold. D'you know what some Captain – one of our people – did to him once? Listen, it'll make you laugh. The whole crew was fed up with him, and they'd stopped off somewhere down this way, some barren island, for coal. Someone told him there were boys ashore, young black boys – that's his weakness. He got dressed up and went ashore, and as soon as he was off the Captain weighed anchor. He was hanging about there for forty days, had to get a job as a greaser on a Norwegian ship to get away. Since then he's had the nickname 'The Consul'— What are you doing? Drinking another one? You're going to undo three years in one watch. Leave a drop for Polychronis."

The wireless officer wiped the sweat from his face, threw away his cigarette and lit another. He started to cough. "They stink, the fu— they're mouldy. This heat! Pour me a drop. The last."

The First Mate poured.

"Women like to sell what they've got. It's in their blood, I tell you."

"And I tell you not to drink any more. You're not used to it."

"Once someone I knew got married to a fine girl. He ate up all her dowry, then he started renting her out to friends. He took out her gold teeth and sold them. He sold the girl herself to some brothel. She died with his name on her lips. She loved him."

"That's normal."

"He loaded her on a cart and sold her for medical students to cut up."

"The bastard."

"Yes. I'm sorry I'm not like him. If you don't sell them, they don't respect you."

"Go and lie down. We'll talk again tomorrow."

"I'm not going anywhere. I'll get it off my chest now. You did well to bring it up."

"What are you talking about? Take it easy."

"Eighteen years old. Wearing a cheap black dress. No, brown. It was a tax-collector who brought her to my ship, the *Aspasia*.

"'She's an orphan,' he told me. 'She's got an uncle in Beirut, a grocer. He's going to look after her. Take her to his shop and hand her over, in the name of charity.'

"I thought about the trouble it would be. Then I looked at her eyes, imploring me. I agreed. Those sharks the mailboat workers, leaning on the rails like carrion crows, looked at her as if she was loukoumi.

I kept them away. When I went on watch I locked her in my cabin. She was still a child. Well-behaved, gentle.

"It happened to be afternoon when we reached Beirut. You know the roads leading to the Place des Canons? Which one should I take? They're all the same. Ironmongers, shops, restaurants, open doors – lots of open doors – and on the steps, or on little stools, black girls, their legs half-open. She kept her eyes down and didn't say a word. Just a couple more side-roads to cross and we'd be in the square; I breathed a sigh of relief. Then a big expensive car blocked the road; a cinammon-coloured limousine. Soon as I saw it I got gooseflesh. The pavement wasn't half a metre wide, we were tight up against the wall. The car stopped next to us. I pushed the girl ahead, but didn't make it; the door opened and blocked the pavement completely, right up to the wall. A stench of mixed perfumes hit my nostrils. 'Courage,' I said to myself, and held the girl's hand tight. Madame Blanche, enormous, and painted like a mask by Ensor, got out with a huge effort, her gold bracelets jangling, precious stones glittering on her fingers. I could smell arak on her breath as she spoke: 'Nikolas, my boy! I'd given you up for lost! You old sod, d'you forget so easily? Get in, let's go straight to Zachlé and look at the mountains!' She grabbed the girl by both cheeks and kissed her on the lips. 'My little dove, why don't you say anything? Come on, then,' and she put her arms round us and pushed us towards the door.

"'Blanche,' I said, begging, almost crying, 'Blanche, I'll see you later; we've got business and we're late.'

"'I'll take you myself, right away.'

"I took her by both hands; 'She's my sister. We have to go.'

"'Three hundred souris cash. Every fortnight, when you come here, I'll pay all your expenses. And whichever girl you fancy, on the house. Got it? Let's go.'

"'As I recall,' I said through my teeth, 'We never did that kind of business. You brought them to me, I never brought them to you. Let us pass.' I could feel the girl's nails digging into my palm. Blanche's eyes rolled, like the beads of a Chinese conjuror under coloured lights. 'All right. But isn't there something you've forgotten, you dog?'

"'I haven't forgotten. But now's not the time for me to pay you back. Step aside, I tell you, or I'll start shouting.'

"'You've got a nerve. One moment, just a word. For the sake of the bed we shared. Come on, Nikolas.'

"I was disgusted. But I remembered the time I was stuck in my cabin with three kilos of stuff. The dealer hadn't come to pick it up, and the police were hanging round just outside, waiting for the order to come in. I remembered how I'd been stitched up and sent down before— four years behind bars— black, foreign prisons— Then Blanche came in. She got the picture at once. 'You're sunk,' she said. 'Give it to me, quickly.' She opened her enormous bosom and put it between her breasts.

"'What're you doing? You know what you're doing? It's—'

"'Shut up, you ox, shut up. Come and collect it this afternoon.'

"She left. The police moved aside to let her pass; smiles and greetings. In the afternoon she handed it over, untouched. We drank some arak. Whether from gratitude, or because in those days she was radiant, shining, I slept with her.

"'I'll never forget you,' I said; 'Whatever you want from me, whenever you want it. We'll bump into each other again.'

"She smiled and patted my cheek. She could lay down the law right through Lebanon and Syria. They say she brought the government down somewhere— anyway—

"'Let's sort it out right now,' she says; 'Give me the girl, she'll be all right in my—'

"'Let me go, Blanche. On the life of your daughter.'

"That made her wild. She stepped back; 'Don't put my daughter's name in your filthy mouth, you ungrateful bastard! Some day you'll be sorry!' She gave me the five fingers with both hands, turned red in the face and got back in the car.

"Night had fallen. We got to the square. We found her uncle's shop straight away, but some black guy there laughed and said the person we were looking for had sold up a month before and gone to Venezuela. 'Address?' the girl asked. 'Oh, in Caracas—' then some customers came in and he left us.

"We went outside and stood looking at each other. It was then I noticed she had beautiful eyes. The tram passed, ringing its bell, on the way to Rue Damas or Bab Idris. Cars going to the Alley, Zachlé or Hamana. A beggar, sitting on the ground, was singing a song that seemed not to come from his mouth, but from all the open doors, all the streets, every mouth. It was the time of day when all the narrow streets from the square down to the sea started to light up and sparkle, as if some hand had turned them on. Green, blue, yellow, cherry-red. Monique, Madama Marika, Chryssa, Malvina, Madame Violette. And over there, if you climbed a palm-tree in the square, to read the stars better, you'd see, among the merry, mixed-up lights, 'Blanche', by the sign of a green fish. It was the time everyone went down to the sea, just as the Phoenicians, wearing short cloaks dyed with brick-dust, had once done. We stood outside the Bohsali pastry-shop and looked each other in the eyes. 'Listen,' I said, "we can both see this is all wrong. I've got the answer—'"

"Hang on, just a moment – listen to the engine – 'Loves me, loves me not—'"

The engine of the *Pytheas* wasn't doing as much as thirty revs. She was making no headway. The First Mate bent to the engine-room voice-pipe. "What the devil are you doing down there? What? They've dropped? Are you telling me?— They're doing it deliberately, the lazy sods. What? Send someone down?— We'll fix them when we get to China— Diamantis? Have I ever asked you to send up one of your greasers to take over the wheel? Eh? Get some steam up, if you have to cut your throats. Wake up the first engineer then, what are you waiting for?— Why ask me?— Oh, do as you like." Swearing, he plugged the voice-pipe with the whistle. "Diamantis, go and wake the Captain and tell him we're going backwards. Hurry." He went into the wheelhouse and stood looking at his watch by the compass-light, counting the engine revs. Silence. The engine con-rods were resting.

Diamantis came back and stood beside him.

"What did he say, boy?"

"He said they're to have five packets of cigarettes, and two bottles of beer each."

"Did he say anything about loukoumi too, eh? Or should we pay the buggers off the day after tomorrow? What a mess. Run down and tell the third officer to wake up a greaser and one of the other cadets."

"What if they don't want to come?"

"Do as I say."

The cadet hurried off.

He turned back to Nikolas, whose head had sunk to his chest as if he were sleeping on his feet. "Are you asleep?"

"No. We seem to be moving."

"Yes, just a bit— why don't you go and lie down?"

"No, I'll get to the end of the story first."

They were silent. Diamantis came back: "The first engineer got them going. He put in a few shovels full himself, and the third officer raked out the ashes. *They* got up and did the job. The others said the salt cod and onions we had last night had upset them."

"Damned if I know what upset them— but between you and me, they're right. What can you do? Call that food we eat? And no refrigerator, not a drop of cold water, or a lemonade. They dump you in a worn-out scow that should have been sold before the war for scrap, for the devil's mother. Coming apart at the seams. O.K. Diamantis; go over to the other side, and take care. Look at the compass from time to time— and tell Polychronis to go down and make us two coffees without sugar."

"I don't want any coffee," the wireless officer muttered, "but if there's a drop of drink—"

"What? Have you drunk the lot, you monster?"

"Finished it just now— It's changed my mood. I'm flying. From the day I gave it up, I turned into a bastard. I got miserable, I got mean."

"But you got well."

"Thanks a lot! Well, let me finish. What's the time?"

"Three."

" 'We'll go back to the ship,' I say to her; 'I'll get the Captain to let us take you back without paying the fare; he's a good chap—'

"Suddenly she changed, in front of my eyes – unrecognizable. She pursed her little lips and said stubbornly 'I'm not going anywhere. You don't know what I went through in Athens. Bad luck all the time. I had to look after my aunt's five children, five wild animals. And the things they called me: ill-bred, lazy, parasite— I'm not going back. I've got a friend in Alexandria.'

" 'You're raving. How will you get into Egypt? Got a visa?'

" 'We'll get one.'

"'What are you saying— you've no idea—'

"'I'll cross in the night.'

"'Not even a cat could get across. We'll go back to Athens.'

"'Never. Over my dead body.'

"Then suddenly she seemed to calm down. She picked at a button on my waistcoat—" the wireless officer stopped a moment and took a deep breath. "Listen, Yerasimos— may the sea rot my shirt and bleach my bones— may I never escape—"

"Enough. I believe you."

"She twisted my waistcoat button with her little fingers. Then she spoke out plain: 'Take me to that friend of yours, the one who stopped us with the car.'

"A whiplash across the face, or being hosed from head to foot with boiling water, wouldn't have hurt me as much. 'What are you saying, child?' I managed to mutter, 'D'you know what you're saying?'

"'She seemed a good woman,' she said cold-bloodedly.

"'She's not a bad woman. But her work's filthy, disgusting. How can I explain—'

"'I understand. I'm not a child. Listen. You'll take me there as a servant. I know how to cook. Just till I find a better job. I've been to school, I can speak French. Just for a few days. When you come back, come and get me out. I'm not going back now.'

"The blood rushed to my head. I felt like slapping her face, but I held back. I grabbed her by the arm; 'Come on, we're going back to the ship.'

"Her eyes flashed. Suddenly she pushed me: 'Let go of me! You can't order me about, you're not my father or my brother. Go back to your ship and leave me alone.'

"I tried to smile. 'Fine, just as you like. Let's go and eat some baklava, and we might think of something better.'

"We crossed the road. I had some idea to get her into the side-streets and force her back to the ship. Then suddenly Vera stopped us. The Russian girl with the sapphire eyes, the high-class one, she was a singer in a second-class cabaret at the time. She'd often talked to me about the works of Aivazofski and Repin. And about Chagall; she'd studied drawing with him in St Petersburg under Bakst. She didn't stop a moment, she just ruffled my hair and disappeared into the crowd. I turned to look at the girl – I hadn't let got of her hand for more than a second – and found I was holding some black guy's dirty hand. He gave me a funny look. I shot off like an arrow into the flood of humanity. I pushed, I hit, I raved. Nowhere. My mind cracked. I went off and drank an arak."

"The best thing to have done would have been to go to the police, or to Blanche's place."

"You're talking like a child. There wasn't time. The police— when you don't know the language. A mess. Beirut— I had a quarter of an hour, and I needed ten minutes just to get to the harbour. I had two or three drinks one after the other and set off down the Rue el Borge. I bumped into the Chios woman. You know her?"

"No. I've heard of her."

"The blind one. Must be a hundred years old; forty years a whore and another forty a madam. Always outside the door of the brothel, winter and summer, sitting on a stool. She recognized me by my cough. 'Bend down,' she said. She ran her hand over my face. 'Nikolas, the good-for-nothing! But why are you crying?'

"That Chios woman, God rest her soul, had a son who was killed in '13, a volunteer in Emin Aya. Her daughter died at twelve, from smallpox. 'Call me mother,' she told me once, 'that's how my Manolis used to lie to me.'

"'So why are you crying?' she says.

"I told her the whole story.

"'You monster! You dog! Worthless! What have you done? What have you done, you Turk?'

"'It wasn't my fault,' I told her. 'I've got to go; the boat's leaving.'

"She grabbed me by the belt and pulled me like a dog. 'And me, boy, why didn't you think of me? Me, who's been searching for a child, on land and sea— I'd have taken her far away from here. I'd have treated her like a princess! Then I'd have had someone to close my eyes for me— Let any woman come to me and say I made her a whore. I take them grown-up and ready, and even then I treat them like my own children. And if some idiot turns up who wants to marry one of them, I give her away. Why am I telling you, Turk-lover, you know it already,' and she started to wail. 'Now you'll never amount

to anything. You threw her into the jaws of the wolf, you blind idiot.'
She lifted up her hands: 'May men bury you and may demons dig you
up! I'd tell it to Charon. I spit on you!'

"I got to the ship as they were pulling up the gangplank. I was on
the eight to twelve; I watched the Sidon light through clouded eyes.
Tyre must have seen me biting my hands from rage and frustration.
Difficult watch; I forced myself through it. When it was over I went to
my cabin and lay down, fully dressed. I felt something hard on the
pillow, under my head. A big tar-paper packet with wax seals. There
were three hundred and fifty souris inside, and a letter that smelt of
'Quelques Fleurs':

> Nikolas. I'm glad you changed your mind. The little dove will
> do well. As soon as you come back, come to me and we'll talk.
> Bon Voyage,
> Blanche.

"I smoked a cigarette with stuff in it and slept like a calf. Three
hundred and fifty souris, Yerasimos. Not two hundred. They told you
wrong. I was twenty years old then— and poor." He wiped away the
sweat that was dripping from his forehead.

"Twenty days later I was back, and I went to see Blanche. She and
her beloved Armenian were sitting on silk cushions, drinking mastic.
She got up and kissed me on both cheeks.

"'I want to talk to you,' I said.

"Avxentis got up and left.

"'Bring me the girl. Right now. Take your money,' and I threw the
packet in her face. She rolled her little fat-buried eyes. With difficulty
she bent down and picked up the packet. Laughing, she said 'The girl's
gone to Damascus. Some pasha took her home with him. A mountain
of luck; she's swimming in gold. I had some expenses, but I got them
back ten times over.' Suddenly her voice hardened. 'What can I tell
you, eh? Fool. Malaka. Too honest. She was a virgin. Didn't you
know enough to stuff her before you sent her to me?'

"I didn't open my mouth. I just stood and listened to her. She
carried on talking fast, and drinking. She laughed coarsely; 'Know
what she said about you? Said I should look to see if you had any—'

"I must have turned red in the face. Suddenly Blanche was sorry for what she'd said and tried to calm me down. Gave me a big glass of whisky. I wanted to go, but I had this full glass. The bottle went down quickly; I don't know— I can't remember— how I found myself in the best room in the house, on top of Adnan, a beautiful Druse girl. And if someone can tell me how the money got to be back in my cabin when we left— Have you got any cognac, something to drink?"

"No."

"Judge me, then. Why don't you say something?"

The bell sounded four double rings.

"Just a minute while I hand over the watch."

Captain Panayis from Lakithra came up, dragging one foot. The First Mate lit the lamp. The second mate's bald head shone red and sweaty, not a single hair on it. He was wearing khaki trousers, slippers, and a sleeveless woollen vest. A sixty-year-old giant. The two of them came out of the wheelhouse and stopped by the wireless officer.

"As I said, Captain Panayis."

"O.K."

"Have a good watch. Let's go, Nikolas."

"Wait five minutes boys, so my eyes can get used to the darkness. Five minutes; I've got something to tell you." He drank off the coffee they'd brought him in one gulp and lit a cigarette, without saying anything.

"Well?"

"What is it? Tell us."

"I had a dream. But what a dream!" He gave a dry cough.

"Tell us, then," said the wireless officer.

"How to explain— I don't know if I ought to tell you. Well, boys, I saw— Damn it!— How— How I was lying down with my sainted mother. Then it wasn't my mother, it was my sister, God rest her soul— Darkness take it!— I still haven't got over it."

"Oh," said Nikolas, "is that all? I've had that one lots of times. It's easy to explain, it's obvious. It's the roots you've got, from your mother's insides, then her breasts. From where you came out, to speak plainly. Then there's the heat, the climate— What did you eat last night?"

"Just some rice pudding. Oh, and a tin of pineapple."

"Ah, bravo! Me, if I eat anything sweet in the evening, on board ship, I dream of my mother, dead."

"Me, too," muttered Captain Yerasimos.

"You too what?"

"Well I've seen myself sleeping with—" and he waved his hand.

"Is there one of our churches where we're going?" asked Captain Panayis.

"Don't know," said the wireless officer, "but there might be a Protestant one."

"I'll light a candle for— forty years dead—"

"Panayis," the First Mate interrupted, "could you do me a favour?"

"If I can."

"Tell us in a few words the story about Aleouta."

"Ooh – it's forty-five years – I've forgotten."

"As much as you can remember. For our countryman here, who's never heard it."

"Well I can't refuse a favour. But don't interrupt me, or I'll lose my place. Well— I was an ordinary seaman then, on a Cuban ship. Very young. We went up North, to some island, for leather." He scratched his head, "I can't remember what it was called— Koska, Kiska— something like that. Cold. You'd piss and it wouldn't reach the ground. Froze in the air. What a port to land up in! A few warehouses with tin roofs. Night all the time. Couldn't sleep on board— We five or six Kephallonians went ashore together. Behind the warehouses we found a little low place with a lamp hanging up and a sign, 'Spirits and Wines, Smoke and Matches.' Didn't say anything about women. Someone dressed in heavy clothes, like an Eskimo, opened the door to us. Huge moustaches hanging down from his wrapped-up face.

"'Sit down Sorrs' he said as if he was swearing at us. We sat on some benches in front of a low table and ordered a bottle. The floor was covered in sawdust. Couple of shelves on the wall, with dusty bottles. He climbed up on a stool to reach them. Slipped, but managed to hang on to the bottle: 'Where did they sow your seed, cuckold Englishman? Shit on the soul of Metland, you and your money and your flag!'

"We fell about laughing. 'Where're you from, Barbar?'"

"'Barbarians and Tunisians cut you up! Kephallonia. Why?'

"He ruined himself treating us, but he never stopped cursing for a moment. He asked us for news of all three hundred and sixty three villages. He'd left at twenty, been all round the world and finished up, an old man, on that island.

"'I'll die here,' he told us. 'I'll never see Deilinata again. They'll bury me in the ice, and I won't rot.'

"'And why don't you go back home?'

"'Because I killed three people in one night.'

"'The law won't touch you after so many years' we told him.

"'Shit on the law,' he shouted; 'Kephallonia has its own law, the law of the knife, and that'll get me. No, I'm not going anywhere.'

"Next day I went on my own. 'Is there a girl at all, Zisimos? Anything doing? I shall burst—'

"He thought a bit— 'There's a place behind here. There's nowhere else. Local woman, does it for small change. Husband's away all night and comes back in the mornings. I mean, you need a watch to check, 'cos this time of year there's no dawn around here. What time are you off?'

"'First thing in the morning.'

"'You won't have time.'

"I found the place easily. I was welcomed by a roaring fire and a stink of leather clothes. Ordered a drink. There were three or four cradles hanging from the low ceiling, and from one of them you could hear a baby crying. She rocked it a little with a stick and the crying stopped. Then the next cradle started to cry. She did the same again, that one stopped. So then the third one started up; what a noise! For half an hour she went from one to the next, till they'd all calmed down, and only then did she bring the bottle I'd ordered. I set my great plan in motion: I spread out five or six gold dollars in front of me on the table and made as if I was counting them. When she bent down to serve me I could just make out her face. Slitty eyes and a small mouth. She smelt of whale-fat, salt fish and untanned leather. She looked slyly at the dollars. It was ages before I could get her to understand. I mean, I think she was doing it deliberately. Finally she made up her mind, and then all the cradles started crying at the same time. One would calm down, then another would go crazy. She started to get undressed. A sealskin coat, a leather jacket. I made gestures to tell her it'd be better to just get undressed from the waist down. She laughed, and explained in broken Russian that to get her yellow waxed-cloth drawers off she'd have to take everything else off, because they were held up by straps over her shoulders, and down by straps under her feet. Hell of a job. 'Do whatever you have to do,' I said.

"She took her time about it. You wouldn't believe it, boys— you couldn't load that many clothes on an ox-cart— And then we heard sleigh-bells in the distance. 'My husband!' she whispered, scared, and started to get dressed, and a lot more quickly, too, which annoyed me. The sleigh-bells faded away. She started to get undressed again, really slowly. Then the cradles started up again. What with those cradles, and the sleighs passing with their bells ringing, and getting dressed and undressed, time passed; it was after midnight. Finally she was standing in front of me naked as the day she was born. What a body! And that moment, just as I started to caress her, the *Dorothea Cuba* started to sound its whistle, over and over again. The she-gorilla jumped up, laughing and clapping her hands. I looked at the door, I looked at the girl. I weighed it up a bit, then fell on her. The cradles screamed, the sleighs passed continually, and the ship never stopped sounding its whistle.

"Then suddenly, boys – I swear by all that's holy to me – one of the roof-beams, either from the heat or the weight of snow on the tin roof, breaks like a cucumber and hits me on the shoulder, then the door bangs open and in comes Zisimos.

"'Clear off, and look sharp!' Then he turns to the she-gorilla, who's covered herself with a blanket: 'Get dressed, you slut! I've had your husband in my shop these three hours, giving him drinks!'

"Well I had a going-over from the Captain I can still remember; he came close to hitting me. There, I've done you the favour you asked."

"You've told it better other times, Panayis," said the First Mate. "What's happened to all that long explanation about the clothes?— You're getting old."

"Just as well. But did I tell you the one about the cabin-boy? It's only short."

"Tell it, tell it," they said together.

"Well, I was Captain on a mailship. Amvrakia to Ionia. It was one night in the Oxies, weather like vinegar. Wind east-south-east, the Sirocco-Levantes. Pylaros and Tzantes on watch. We hadn't seen a light, and I was sitting up on the bridge with the second officer, waiting for it to clear up, when I hear lots of noise and shouting from the companionway down to the First Class. I went down slowly and stood in the gangway by the cabins. The passengers were shouting 'Cabin-boy! Cabin-boy!' In a corner I saw the boy on duty – young chap, new to the sea – crouched down low, throwing up and shouting 'Passengers! Passengers!' He panicked as soon as he saw me: 'Don't throw me off, Captain! Don't get rid of me, my mother's a widow! I'll get used to it, I will!'

"'It's all right boy, I won't sack you. But tell me, why are you shouting at the passengers?'

"'Same reason they're shouting at me: I need help just as much as they do, Captain.'"

"Well, have a good watch, and if the engine-room messes you about, call the Captain. We've done sixteen miles in the last four hours, damn it."

"Call him, eh?" muttered the old man. "What should I call him?— You're pulling my leg, Yerasimaki, but that's O.K. I used to call him to make me a coffee, now I call him to give me orders."

"He used to be a sailor under you, I suppose."

"Yes, on a Belgian ship. A sailor!— you'd have to force him to do his watches. By the time he'd lifted one foot up, the other had gone rotten. Like a mule. And he never learnt to tie knots or splice. Always picking his nose, just like he does now."

"They say he used to pick a few other things, too," said the First Mate.

"Oh, don't ask me about those sorts of things, I wouldn't know. Got no interest in the other thing, myself. Look! The sun's wearing horns! It'll be hot today. Cheers; thanks for the company."

They went down the companionway and stopped on the deck. "Don't light another one," said the First Mate; "You're poisoning yourself. Time to sleep."

"Well?" said the wireless officer, looking at the deck.

"Well what?"

"But— what we were talking about, the girl, Beirut—"

"Ah—Yes. You were right. Wasn't your fault. I didn't know; forgive me."

"Oh, it doesn't matter. Are you sleepy?"

"A bit. Why?"

"We could sit here, where it's cooler."

"You've got some stamina! We'll wear ourselves out. It's not good to stay up all night. And in seas like this, it's death."

"You're afraid of death?"

"Just like everyone else."

"I'm curious. Wonder what it's like?"

"What a thing to talk about at this hour! We'll talk again tonight." He made to leave, but hesitated. "Tell me— did you see the girl again? Did you find her?"

"No. Never."

"I'm off."

The wireless officer was alone. He lit a cigarette and took a deep drag. There was a cold sweat on his forehead. He knelt down, bent his head over the rail, put two fingers down his throat and threw up into the sea.

Part 2

Sixth Watch

> *Portrait of a man.*
> *A la Comtesse Ariane de Jacquelin Dulphé.*

You can't see more than a metre ahead. Half a metre, less, nothing. Less than nothing. It's been coming down since very early. Fog has its own smell, just as rain, typhoon, or any other bad weather does. How it smells! Fills my nostrils, but I couldn't say— Judith! You're ten thousand miles from Gomel and five from me. You're breathing the sweat of Tasman. I'm sure you've forgotten that night on the deck of the *Cyrenia*, off the Minikoi light. You were wearing the night. Your purple dress fell in rags to your feet, your slim feet with palm-frond sandals. You kicked it away and it was lost in the scuppers, behind the lifeboat. Only the green of your eyes moved.

"Put your dress on. Cover yourself. Please, put it on."

"The monsoon's taking it, don't you see?"

"You're like a naked Chinese sword-blade."

"I want my scabbard."

Judith! Everything has its own smell.

But not people. They steal theirs from things. Your red hair smells like the hold of the *Pinta* when it came back from its first voyage. The narrow streets of the ghetto— "Streets are not safe at night. Avoid all saloons." Chagall's *Arch-Rabbi*.

"Hey, innocence! Kiss me."

"Another time. When I've got the taste back."

"You've lost it? Where?"

"In Barbados, in the sand. I left it on the lips of a black girl."

"Fine, then bite me. To hurt."

60

"No teeth. I left them in an unripe mango, over there, opposite Cochin."

"Feel me."

"Judith— With what hands? I lost my sense of touch on the faded silk of an armchair in some house in Iquique— there— and a sapphire with it, a big sapphire."

"Then look me in the eyes. Why do you keep yours cast down? Look at me!"

"They're not mine. An old beggar in Volos wears mine; we swapped."

"Look at me with his."

"He was blind. A girl led him around by the hand."

"Let me lead you by the hand."

"Yes."

"Let's go. I'm cold."

"Wait. Let me tell you a fairy tale."

"No, let's go in."

"It's hot inside. The fan's broken. It smells like a chemist's shop. The sheets are dirty, the basin stinks. There's a scorpion running up the walls, and I'm afraid."

"Of the scorpion?"

"Of you."

"Let's go in, I say."

"Take your hands away. Tell me more."

"Well— Everyone was asleep except old father Jehu. He was reading by the lamp with the smoky chimney. He was reading the big book. They smashed the door off its hinges. I was twelve years old. I hadn't finished brushing my red hair. There were twelve of them, with black crosses on their arms. Drunk. Then— in front of my mother, in front of Jehu, who was praying with his eyes closed—"

"And the twelve men?"

"I don't remember. I've never been with another man. But tonight— Not because I like you. Just out of curiosity. Let's go in."

"Tomorrow, in Colombo."

"Now."

"Give me your hand. You'll trip. There's a step. Don't turn on the light— You know— I'm sick."

"I don't care."

"Listen— it's as if we're breaking up the game to steal the prize."

"I want to wear your skin. To steal something from you."

"Do what you like. Steal whatever you find. But show it to me first—"

And that's how it was, like the time I caressed a nude by Pascin – in front of three museum guards, and they didn't see me.

You can't see a hand's breath off the bow. The First Mate's complaining. It's getting thicker all the time. He complains, and spits. His cigarette's damp and won't draw. Every now and then he pulls the wire of the steam-whistle. Its chimney belches and bellows for five seconds, then for fifty-five it's dumb again. He cocks his ears to starboard, to port, ahead. He cups his hands round them. There's another whistle calling, you can just hear it. Polychronis, the look-out, is standing right up in the bows, and when the whistle of the *Pytheas* stops he sounds the fog-horn. It's getter nearer— I can hear it off to starboard now.

Another whistle. Then dead silence. Then the sound of the other one, bearing down.

"Be ready!" he shouts to the helmsman: "When I tell you 'Hard-a-starboard' or 'Hard-a-port' you turn with it. Got that?"

"Yes."

He thinks to himself— "Just our luck Diamantis should get sick. He's running a fever. Who sent him off to catch the pox? Lucky there are new medicines now—" He pulls the whistle-wire. "Leave you— new. And us? We've got nothing new here. All rotten. My grandfather used to sound the whistle like this, in the fog. Radar, depth-sounder— What luck!— They send you out a young man— Diamantis will get away with it, but we went rotten. Mercury—"

He blows the whistle again.

Diamantis is lying in his bunk. He's afraid. He's covered in spots. "Are they from the heat? But the fever?" He hears the whistle. He remembers the woman, her white dress, which she didn't take off, just lifted. The rust-dark hairs— He pulls off the sweat-soaked sheet and kicks it away. Her eyes; kind and willing. The cadet smiles, feels easier. "If she'd had anything, she'd have told me. Like the girl in Lome."

His mother. Suffering, wearing black. His over-filled sailor's kit-bag was leaning outside, by the flower-bed with the basil. His sister cut a carnation and gave it to him. Then he set off. His mother didn't weep. In their island, women never weep in front of others. Weeping is like undressing, and worse. They weep at night, when the oil runs out in the lamp and the wick sputters. When the smell of burnt oil gets you by the throat. "Diamantis," she'd said in her hoarse voice, "Be sensible. Look after yourself—." And she'd whispered in his ear. They loaded the kit-bag on the little cart. The tears started as they passed the last house in the village.

"Could it be scabies?— Another two days— Everything goes wrong. Heavy seas ahead— They're not making much steam— Now the fog— From now on I'll take care. I'll get my papers, we'll get my little sister married—"

He stares at the ceiling. A seam crosses the plates at an angle. He shuts his eyes— "If there's an even number of rivets, then I haven't got anything.

"One— two— four— eight— twelve. Even. Maybe I miscounted?" He counts again— "Twelve. Right." He smiles.

He gets up and goes to the washroom, naked as the day he was born. The water's off at that hour. It'll be back on in the morning, eight to ten. He knows there's no water. He twists the tap. Then he goes and lies down on his bunk for a while. He gets up again and straightens his father's photograph, which has fallen sideways. He stands on his bunk and counts the rivets again, touching each one with his finger. "Twelve— again."

He drops down and falls asleep with the light on.

Captain Panayis tosses and turns in his bunk. He hears the whistle. "Fog. Just like then. I wasn't on the bridge— I'd gone for a piss and before I'd even started we'd ridden up on the Dutchman— Crashed into him— If I'd had Yerasimos for First Mate—"

Still lying down, he searches the floor with his hand. He finds a bottle, turns and pisses into it.

He passes his hand along the wall, looking for something— "Ah! There it is." A tiny bell gives a double ring. "Oh, three hours sleep left." He starts to snore.

"Dead ahead!" Polychronis shouts from the bows. "Coming close."

"Hard-a-starboard!" the First Mate orders the helmsman, and gives one long pull on the steam-whistle. "How's it looking?"

"She's right alongside," the helmsman answers.

A hoarse whistle came from the other ship; she too had ordered "All starboard".

"Straighten up. Don't want to catch each other by the stern."

"Wheel's in the centre," says the helmsman.

"Take a look, boy: it's all black out there, a whole island of black. Turn your wheel to port."

"Port."

"And a bit more, Thanasis— Well, could have been worse. The other one's got no radar either. They've got it on the mailships. No-one worries about the crews." He wipes his forehead with his left hand and lights a cigarette. "Weather'll clear up again at dawn."

"Captain Yerasimos, telephone!"

"Yes? Weather report? Say it's clearing up. Just now— You busy?— Fine— I'm soaked— In Kifissia?— What made you remember?— Oh, come on— Yes— It'll be cool— Good for them. Go and grill yourself black then. Bye." He pulls the wire for the steam-whistle again. When can I rest a little?— A plate of cabbage— Dig a bit, plant something, watch it grow— Sea all the time, watches all the time— it's unnatural. Are we fish? Oh, to the devil with it. And they wrap you in sailcloth, he says, and weigh you down. Then splash, off the stern— no priest. "As far as I'm concerned", he says, "the dogs can drag me off when I die; I won't feel it"— "How d'you know?" He pulls the whistle again. He's a sod, that Nikolas— "I believe," he says, "When I'm afraid." I shit on his belief.

Polychronis came and stood beside him.

"Why have you left the bows, boy?"

"To relieve Thanasis, and make coffee. It's all clear, I can't hear anything."

"O.K., off you go. Hurry up. And bring a few coffee-beans for chewing." He sounds the whistle again— And a woman ... to lie down, smoking, and watch her coming and going, singing, complaining— He can say what he likes; women are faithful creatures. God's joy.

Forgetting the whistle, he goes and leans against the brass engine-room telegraph— "What d'you say?"

"The coffee."

"Oh. Put it there. Thanasis, have a few beans to chew, so you don't fall asleep. And you, crazy Polychronis, keep your mind on the wheel." He pulls the whistle once more, and stands thinking to himself—

Sales Terriens ...

The wireless cabin is buzzing with atmospherics; only the sound of the billowing smoke-stack drowns then out. The noise and heat are unbearable.

He's sitting in front of the receiver, elbows on the table and hands over his eyes. The receiver's talking in its own language. About twenty ships working, audible at five hundred miles, and the shore stations.

De VJR ... XXX man overboard ... approximate position ... please all ships in vicinity keep sharp look-out.

He wrote it in the log. Smiled bitterly. "Keep sharp look-out." Night and fog. Even if it were daylight – straight into the jaws of the shark like a dead dog. The sailor's fate. One of them followed us from Suez as far as Aden. Another from Aden to Colombo. And the hungry one that's with us now, that joined us at Sabang, will leave us off Santoun.

"And how d'you know it's a different one each time?" some landsman asked me once, joking. "D'you tell them apart by their neckties?" Idiot— just the same as you can tell from a distance the tram that'll take you home.

On a cargo ship once, when they'd pulled out a shark, I saw the heart, cut out from its body, still beating in a bucket of sea-water, splashing and spraying. The game carried on for half an hour before it slowed down and stopped. Who could you tell that to and they'd believe you?

"Man overboard," the set repeated.

Just a moment. He fell off the Indian ship. He'll be black, then. He'll have escaped. They'll only eat blacks by mistake.

Remember the black kids in Aden and Djibouti, swimming next to them?

"But how could they tell at night?"

At night, arsehole landsman, the smell says the colour.

When you hook a shark, never pull it on deck alive. It can hurt you, tear you open, kill you. Hit it on the head right away. Come here and let me tell you something in your ear, but don't tell anyone, they'll think you're a fool. You can overcome the fiercest shark with a bucket of fresh water. You can kill it. Throw it in its eyes and mouth. They never go near rivers, not even river-mouths. They'll leave you alone if they see muddied waters.

"Lies! In that case why won't the whites swim outside the wire net in the river Chat el Arab in Basrah?"

Because there's a stream, idiot. A sea-current that goes a long way up, and they follow it. Don't you believe me? Make the journey and you'll see it with your own eyes.

"I adore seagulls," some lovely girl told me once; "Proud birds."

What are you saying, child— land-creatures like yourself. They go to sea to eat. As soon as they feel rain, they go and roost in the harbours. When there's a dolphin playing off the bow, the gulls mob it, they peck out its eyes, tear it apart and eat it ... Coastal birds. I know some birds the size of your little finger; you see them out on the ocean and they won't come and rest in the rigging.

I get dizzy on dry land. The most difficult journey I ever made, the most dangerous, was on asphalt, from Syntagma to Omonia. I've thrown up ashore, in Lebanon, the same way land people throw up in a sea-breeze. You're sorry for us because we have no home, because we walk with a sailor's roll, because in port we wear unironed clothes, crumpled shirts. I'm happy for you: a safe bed, peaceful sleep. Coffee on the bedside table, newspapers. A little excursion at the weekend, to go and eat meat-balls. But I wouldn't change my job for yours, not even for a day.

"Tell us a tale from your travels ..." How many times I've heard that. What for? So you can nudge each other and snigger?

The First Mate's sounding the whistle. Good sailor. Looks ahead, always ahead. Doesn't look you in the eyes; asks you something and keeps watching the sea. "Tell me," he said suddenly the other day, "where's your father buried?" "How should I know? I was at sea when he died."

Child of Manchuria ... When he first went to Tien Tsin at seventeen years old the local Chinese had given up smoking opium all the time, but they were more drunk than ever. What were they getting? Kouropatkin, the victualler ... They'd creep down to his tent at night. On the box he used for a table, tucked in a slice of bread, a cockroach, a huge monster. "I'll shoot you at dawn," and he picked it up, took a good look at it, put it in his mouth and swallowed it. "Best quality sultanas! Here's to your island!" Kouropatkin had more trouble keeping away from laughter than my father did keeping away from the Captain. "Bugger off!" he'd say; "And next time you won't get away with it!"

A pack of cards would talk in his hands. He opened a bar in Leo Yan, and made enough to buy a bakery in Moukden ... When he was twenty he came back with Vragel's troops. Five thousand drachmas and a box of sweets in his pocket. Started to travel— Constantinople, Smyrna, Piraeus, Alexandria, Brindisi— Came one night with a hand-cart loaded with gold and silver coins from Turkey. Gave us a handful each, and in a month he'd had it all back off us. "Whatever you give me, boys, I'll bring back turned to gold." – My mother used to shake her head.

When I was eighteen I told her I was going to be a sailor. "Be what the devil you like," she said, "Just don't be an informer or a queer." She thought for a bit— "Well there are good men who're queer— honest people. But an honest informer you won't find anywhere."

Day before he died, when the nurse came to tidy him up, he grabbed her by the— Knock it off, Yerasimos, in the name of God! Stop it! My head's splitting! ... Where's he buried? The box with his bones got left in an ouzeri in Ayios Dionysios ... that crafty sexton had been paid to swap boxes. Mother waiting at the gangplank for her son, to carry his bones back to Kephallonia to lie in peace. She realized about the swap, but she didn't say anything. Never even asked. Eight years in China had taught her when to keep her mouth shut.

"I hope they forget my bones in a bordello," he said, "and the girls can use them for flutes, tobacco-pipes and douche tubes."

Oh, stop pulling that damned wire! ... What thief of a priest, what whoreson priest, will read over my body? Yerolymos from Zola? How many years ... in Dili ... in Kupang ... No, in Bali. Somewhere down there, where we were laid up on the *Argonaut* with damaged steering gear.

Another message.

> TTT ... Medical advice ... Sailor of twenty five ... fever forty one ... probably of contageous water ... any ship with doctor please advise ...

That's the *Macao*

As ... QRX ...

I'm thirsty. What's got into me? Like that time on the *City of Djeda*. Some helmsman had got sick with typhus. We were coming up from Bombay. We'd isolated him in a cabin in the bows. Two of us taking it in turns to watch him at night. I was on at midnight. Monsoon on the bow. I gave him camphor and put vinegar compresses on his head. He was quiet. My watch passed and no-one came to take over. The weather had got worse; tons of water running fore to aft. I changed Reginald's compress. His forehead was icy, and he was smiling, with his eyes wide open. Mouth all twisted. I couldn't have left him. One moment it seemed he was opening and closing his eyes, he next he was dribbling from the mouth, then his hand seemed to shake. That was the first time I ever drank. I put some sugar in a bottle of surgical spirit ... What medicine! ....

And again tonight ... What the devil did that drink smell of? What does it remind me of? How did it smell ... Arak ... that's how Blanche's mouth stank.

"Did you see Blanche again?"

— Yes, twelve years later, in Beirut again. I was on the *Corinthia*. She came and stood in the doorway of my cabin. She hugged me, and kissed me on both cheeks like she used to. Something not quite right about the way she talked. "She'll be drunk," I thought.

"I've brought you my daughter. Remember how you used to play with her as a baby? How she pissed on you once? Here she is!"

The girl blushed. About sixteen years old. She was wearing the big white cloak of the Sisters of Saint Joseph. "I'm going to look round the ship," she said, and went off.

Blanche started to cry. First time I'd ever seen her cry; it confused me. "She's leaving me. She's going to a nunnery in Po. They've corrupted her, the filthy cows. But she'll learn something. I got her a first-class ticket, but no bed, the ship's full. For the sake of our old friendship, Nikolas, do what you can to look after my child. Make sure nothing bad happens to her. Did you see how thin she is?"

"She'll sleep in my cabin," I told her; "What more d'you want?"

"And you?"

"Me? Oh, I'll find somewhere."

She took my hand and squeezed it. Burst helplessly into tears. Her make-up dissolved and ran off the corners of her lips, all over my bunk.

"Come on," I said, "Why all this fuss? You can go and see her whenever you like. She might change her mind and come back. Cheer up!"

Then Blanche, madam of the House of Mirrors in Beirut, another in Aleppo and another in Damascus, whose fat arms, when she lifted them up, jangled with five rows of gold bracelets, valued at twenty thousand lires, Blanche, who used to be able to talk day and night without stopping, heaved herself up with difficulty, came up close to me, very close, face to face, opened her mouth, and stuck out her tongue. What was left of it, after the illness and the radium.

I didn't take the smallest step back, I didn't show the slightest sign of shock. "Why don't you go to Paris?"

"I've just come back."

"You'll get better," I said, "bit by bit."

She interrupted me: "Don't try and comfort me. I'll just say one thing: if it's a sin for women to go with men, then it serves me right! I'm well punished. I'm cursed—" She crossed herself.

"And your place?"

"I closed it. Two months ago. I asked Vera – remember her? – to take it over, but she didn't want to."

"Vera! ... Where's Vera now?"

"Dead. A month ago. She drank curare. She'd grown old badly. And such poverty ... But she was proud. She wouldn't take so much as a plate of food from my hands. She hated me." – She hesitated a second – "And you hate me too."

"Me? If it hadn't been for you, that time with the stuff ..."

"You still hold it against me ... for that girl from Mytilene. It wasn't my fault, that's the way she wanted it. I put her to work in the kitchen and I found her in bed. She wanted it ... You turned against me then."

"Listen Blanche, I don't remember anything about all that. Is the Armenian guy, Avxentis, still with you?"

"No, he left. Never mind, he was no good. Well— look after the girl as you would your own eyes."

"Bye. I'll treat her as if I were her brother. Her father."

She took my hand and made as if to kiss it; I pulled it away quickly.

"You said 'Like her father.' – well, you said it." She leant to whisper something in my ear. ... "I'm going ... can I kiss you, or do I disgust you?"

I took hold of her head and kissed her on the mouth. Mouth to mouth ...

"I'm going. I'll go and say goodbye to the girl."

I followed the scene from a distance. Her daughter bore her kisses looking away, indifferent; no tears. The loudspeaker shouted "All visitors ashore."

She was the last off. Night had fallen. The police and customs men greeted her, laughing cruelly, as she passed. I watched her car disappear behind the customs house. Her daughter was laughing, playing with two children. The lights of Beirut came on— the palm-trees ...

A confusion of heat, fog, exhaustion and the noise of the ship's whistle.

Get undressed; I'll give you the fog for clothes ... I'll drink one more, for the sake of the sea ... for the sake of the mermaid on my arm, who jumps in the sea every night, and makes me a cuckold with Poseidon. She comes back in the morning, when I'm asleep, covered in stinging sea-weed. When we stay on land too long she fades, loses her colours ... A little house in the country. To sleep in one night every two years. With no woman beside you. To set sail again in the morning ... the thump, thump of the engine again, the smell of the launch, of the steam – the cook cutting his finger-nails with the kitchen knife. Watch after watch, a bunk full of bugs, repairs, the smell of hot tar, cleaning out the tanks, turbid water to wash in. Water with lion's hairs, river-water, dirtied by crocodiles. Filthy words with our meals, burnt rice pudding, blasphemy for morning greetings, the sickness of the scow. A pull at your big toe to wake you for your watch. Weigh anchor, drop anchor. Crossing sea-lanes ...

Change of watch. Put the batteries on charge. A drink? ... A la Cassa de Lautrec. And now music. A Chinese song. Or further back ... Boléro. A fly, buzzing around in a glass ball that changes colour. Europe; worn out.

Who will forgive me? Alevizos, in Kupang, No ... buried years ago, in Bali.

With the *Argonaut*. We were held up there, damage to the steering-gear. I wasn't more than seventeen years old. Early morning; I was shaving in my cabin. Through the door I saw the palm-trees, motionless, and a light that bathed the land and the sea. A light I found again, years later, in Delos, another early morning ...

Bali!

Then a noise like a roaring fire on the ship: "A son of a whore— a worthless sod— a cuckold ... a thief like me, that's what I want, one of my countrymen!"

I didn't know the voice. I coughed through the soap-froth. "Here I am," I shouted; "What's up?"

"I want – I want, you fart-plug, oregano and garlic. And if you've got it, a bit of parsley. And I want it now!"

I went to the steward and got what he wanted. He took it with trembling hands and brought it up to his nose. He sighed. Old, skinny, with a big brown tobacco-stained moustache and bushy brows that hid his eyes. Wearing a filthy ragged silk shirt and an old cap. "I'll pick you up at sunset and take you to my farm for dinner."

"No," I told him.

"Snakes and a singleside strike you between the eyes. Be ready."

He came before dark. "Are you ready?"

"Yes, hang on, I'll bring a bottle of whisky."

"Bring both your cuckold's horns. Come on."

We got in a little narrow boat. I wet my hand in the water and wiped my forehead.

"What are you doing, you heiffer, you upright pig? Put your hands in your pockets if you don't want to lose them; there are swordfish."

We landed. "We'll walk now, so you can see the place."

On the way, local people, men and women, greeted him, smiling: "To hell with your God, Alevizos," said one; "To hell with the mother of your God," the next; "To hell with your honour" a bit further on. He'd reply with worse curses; I laughed.

"Don't laugh, you lunatic, or I'll take you straight back where I found you."

As we walked along, flocks of crows flapped about like paralytic sponge-fishers and got tangled up in our feet. He bent down and stroked them. We crossed a little wooden bridge into a big space with a broken-down bungalow in the middle. Three young girls, stark naked, greeted us at the door. I stopped and started at them. Suddenly he pushed me and I found myself sitting in a rocking-chair. An enormous snake fell out of the roof onto my knees and I started yelling.

"I spit on you, you shitter— Christodoulos, come here, let me feed you." The snake wrapped itself round Alevizos's body. "He's my child, I've had him fifteen years. He sleeps with me."

The girls brought some big bowls and washed our feet. We sat down to eat; the chicken stuck in my throat: I was looking slyly first at one girl, then at another.

"Eat, boy. You can screw all three later, but first you must get your strength up."

A pure white parrot with a yellow comb strutted about the table, continually shitting on the cloth.

"Does it put you off?" he said. "I'll chuck him out if you like. Out, Mourlodionysis."

"Oh, leave him," I said; "But why doesn't he talk?"

"He's been sulking since morning. I hit him with a spoon because he was chasing Christodoulos. How's the food?"

I couldn't answer because one of the girls was bending down to serve me and her nipple was tickling my eye.

There were coffee and cigars after dinner.

"Shall we go for a walk? The village has more beauties than these here."

"Oh— I'm sleepy. I'd rather rest a bit."

I went and lay down and waited. Just as he'd said, all three came to me. There was a flute playing somewhere outside. From time to time I'd hear a roaring in the distance, and once or twice a long, low whistle, when the girls would get to their knees, frightened: "Nayia, Nayia!"

The four of us lay on our backs, smoking, looking at the stars shining through the big windows; stars so close you could catch them in your hands and juggle with them. Then Namila started to sing and Loana to play some instrument I couldn't see. Talora carried on smoking. Now and then I stroked her knees; in a little while she fell asleep.

I got up and went and looked in Alevizos's room. He was sitting cross-legged on a mattress, chewing on an empty black coral cigarette-holder. Next to him burnt an oil-lamp with three wicks. In his hands an almanac from 1912. He was wearing just his underpants. Round his neck a long brass chain, ending in a medallion that was hidden between his thin, stick-like legs. The snake slept beside him on a silk cushion. Salt fish and dried octopus hung from the walls and ceiling.

"Welcome, genius," he said. "You'll be thirsty, and you've got a right to be. You've been having a wild time with those girls. Kick one of them and tell her to bring drinks, pineapples and mangoes."

"Better not," I said, "they're asleep."

"The sluts!" he roared; "And you're sorry for them, you pig?" he shouted and they came, frightened, to the door. "Little parasites! If you screwed all the fires of St John they wouldn't satisfy you, you little piglets!"

They brought fruit whose scent would make you dizzy.

"When you get back to Greece, send me some books. Church books. And a priest's stole."

"How many years have you been here, Barbar Alevizos?"

"Barbarians and Tunisians! Fifty. And don't ask questions, because you won't get answers. Maybe you think I've hidden myself away down here because of some woman? Ha, ha, ha!" and he started coughing. He made a filthy gesture; "You can't block women up. They're just holes, nothing but holes. Go and sleep for a couple of hours, I'm sick of the sight of you. You're green, like a lizard."

"It's the climate," I said nervously.

"What climate, boy? Best in the world! Go and sleep."

I went, but he called me back. "Hang on. I want to ask you something. D'you smoke hashish?"

"When I get the chance, I don't refuse it."

He lit two cigarettes. He drew deeply on one, made as if to say something, but swallowed the words. The smoke rose to the ceiling in a single puff, without spreading. A distant shrill cry, turning to weeping, reached the room.

"Aina's giving birth," he said, as if to himself. "Another mule who'll be pissing on my trousers in a year or so ... Well, what were we saying? Yes, if you like, stay here. If you feel like it ... You could work on my place. Easy work. You'd keep an eye on the plot and sleep with all the women in the island from nine years old upwards. See? And when I die, everything I've got ..." His head fell gently, as if he were making his confession. He started to snore. I was left to gaze now at the snake, which was stirring, now at Alevizos. Then Mourlodionysis the parrot burst in like a cannon-shot. He leapt on Alevizos and pecked his underpants, tugging at them and blaspheming; the lowest ruffian would have blushed. He changed to "Christ is risen, Christ is risen," then back to blasphemy. Finally he got fed up, settled on Alevizos's legs, and fell asleep.

I went back to the girls. At dawn I got up and bathed in a barrel. The three girls shone in the light, their hair dripping water onto their bodies. They never stopped talking and laughing among themselves. They brought me coffee. I looked across the water at the *Argonaut*, paint flaking, waiting there like a wounded beast ...

Alevizos came. "Well ... you're going?"

"Yes." I tried to make out his eyes, but again I couldn't catch them. The three black girls surrounded him; "She-horses," he muttered. He turned to me: "Well ... I wish you all the best." He gave me his big bony hand.

"Go to the devil!" the parrot screeched. "Go to the devil's mother, go to pieces, go where no-one comes back!" It shocked me, and I stopped dead.

"Go on, off you go. Good wishes are bad luck."

Before I crossed the river I turned my head and watched Alevizos wiping his forehead with a big smoker's handkerchief. "If you change your mind," he called, "Come back whenever you like. I'll be waiting for you," and he waved.

Three years later I met a Greek ship's provisioner in Jacaranda. I asked him about Alevizos. He made a face. "In the five days it took him to die, he mimicked all the birds and animals. Just before that he'd called all the blacks round him and showed them a petrol-tin full of gold. 'It's yours,' he said, 'but wait till I'm gone.' He buried it somewhere on his land – five hundred acres. The blacks are still digging ... Shit on his soul. About two years before he died he went mad. There were germs in his head ... he used to put on priest's robes and burn incense all night, recite psalms with the parrot. The fucker— he left a hundred lires each to his slaves and made them swear to go to his grave once a week and piss on it. Did you know him well?"

Before I could answer, the Captain called him away. Who will forgive me? ...

In Beirut, outside the customs house, just a few days after Blanche died. You got down from a big sky-blue car. You were wearing a khaki safari-suit and a traveller's cap. Two loaded camels, one kneeling each side of you. Your eyes hard, your face tanned by the

Khamsin, Haboub, Samal, Monsoon ... Maria! Impossible, I must be dreaming.

"Demain ... Demain ... C'est promis ..."

Forgive me, forgive me. But don't look in my eyes ... it's not my fault.

"Don't stare at me like a moron! ... You're paler. Still the same stripes, the same clothes ... Bravo! How you've progressed! What? Don't make me laugh! You weren't even fit to sell a packet of duty-free Number Ones ... you missionary, you .... Give me a cigarette."

Her hands trembled as I lit it. She gave an order to the blacks, in their own language, and they took her trunks aboard. She went into the stateroom and stood in front of the mirror, tidying her hair. "Come in, then, why are you standing in the doorway like a bouabis? Order something to drink— two dry martinis."

"I don't drink," I murmured.

She turned and looked at me: "If you were ever worth anything, it was because you used to get drunk."

She drank off in one the drink the steward brought and ordered another. She'd opened a suitcase and was looking for something; her tongue never stopped. "Sit down then, why are you standing up? What were we saying? Yes— I got away from the Bey a treat. I was bored with Syrian sweets, and his tastes— I joined a cabaret in Damascus. Then I ran off. Went to Basrah, but I couldn't stand the climate. I was three months in a 'House' in Oka. Then I went to Marmagoa in Cochin. Crossed over to Kalgan, with a caravan. Went from Osaka to Frisco in a yacht ... Is it true the Meltemi's going to blow? The sea's the only thing I could never get used to ... what a joke ... I saw you one evening in Buenos, in the Calli Pichincha, and I waved to you. You didn't recognize me; you chose some Chilean with no eyebrows, thin as bamboo. What taste ... I went back East, Aden, Hadramout. There was a war on; beautiful men. Radiant. I stayed with the leader of a tribe, in a tent spread with carpets, for two years. We changed places like you'd change a shirt. And Soukan, I loved him – slim, like a woman. One night the Headman would sleep with me, the next with Soukan, and then I'd go to Soukan after midnight, when the old man had had enough, dried up. When he caressed me on the shoulders, like that, down to the elbows ... like that ... do it ... you don't fancy it, O.K ... So I'm going back to Greece loaded with gold. I'm going to get married. I want to have a child, a boy— to rock him to sleep, to bring him up. Does that seem strange to you? I don't tell people of course, but I'm pushing thirty-five. My legs are ruined. Steel and flames. But what would you know?"

She pulled something out of her suitcase; "Ah, here it is. I got it for you. Take it!" She threw it and I caught it in mid-air. A book, bound in velvet, gold lettering on the spine: *Robinson Crusoe.*

"But what's up with you, then? Idiot!" She stroked my hair, and closed the door ...

Still Life with Fruit.
For Ismini, and Thomas Politis.

"Did you get it? We're half-dead down there, it's hell in the stokehold. I turned your ventilator round; why don't you go and lie down?" Tsabournas, the greaser, stands there half-naked, filthy, smiling.

He doesn't answer, just opens a drawer and gives him a wrinkled apple. The greaser bites it, hesitates ... "Don't forget what you said— old, it doesn't matter, whatever's ready to throw out. My old lady fixes them up for the kids."

He nods.

"And that suit you told me about ..."

"Yes. Tomorrow for sure."

"D'you want anything, water, coffee?"

"No."

He wipes his forehead with his scarf and goes.

Yes ... something stinks. Like a cess-pit. I don't feel well; I can hardly see. Something's knocking outside ... five knocks ... Remember the five voyages to Australia ... if I could tell one from the other ... The first; the girl on the *Basedow.* The second ... no ... Yes. The sea, phosphorescing four hours long in the Gulf of Aden ... Aden. Split rocks ... Fucken place ... all the years of travel, I was never afraid of anything as much as that rock, with Kephallonian boys playing hide-and-seek round its damned black roots. Where did you go, child of Paris, to wash away your sins? ... Steamer Point. The museum with the live mermaids. "And no water." And that ragged island at the harbour mouth, with the lazaretto: three bamboo huts with asbestos roofs. As if I could forget ... And the Scottish nun ... the girl with the red cheeks, who'd gone to work there, in memory of Cyril.

I'd like to see Port Said again. The canal office, Simon Arzt's shop, the trees. See the freighters coming back from the South and anchoring to wait. Naked northern sailors, bodies scratched and torn, leaning on the rails ... happy to be coming back, one more time ... Shall I do it? Shall I go back? ... It's another Port Said you see on your way south. Nothing for a sailor but prickly heat powder, fruit salts and quinine. Bloody quinine, and lemons that'll rot half way through the Red Sea. And crabs that stink of mud ... Maybe she was the last woman I'll ever have? ... How many have thought that and been afraid? ... I'm not the only one. There are others, but they don't talk about it ... I've seen it in their eyes. If you expect seamen to talk to you, to open their hearts, you're going too far ... Truth sulks, hides itself. We tell it now and then alone, to ourselves, and even then we're afraid.

It's not the sea that scares us. We command it, and it commands us. No-one knows how to travel it the way the Greeks do. And the Bougazians, the Marmarans, the Black Sea people. And islanders. Tortured faces, torn hands. Moaners and complainers. You who've learnt knots and splices. Give them a ship just off the stocks, they'll know it inside and out within one watch, and in two they'll have changed its character. Throw them into the worst weather, they'll go around bare-headed. The strangest seas, the most difficult, they'll push the pilots and charts aside. "Always sleep with your door hooked open," Barbar Michaelis, a bosun from Spetses, told me once. "In a collision, an explosion, doors seize and won't open. And keep your matches close by." I laughed. "Shut up, boy," he said, and made the five fingers at me; "You're not afraid, boy, because you've never seen your own arsehole." He died in the geriatric ward in Piraeus, looking out at the dusty trees. Died ... and I'll die too. When? Not tonight. We're near land, I can smell it. I've got a few years yet ... harbours ... No other way. The alleyways of San Lorenzo, Genova, Rue Bouterie ... now they live only in Dignimont's pencil, and in my mind. Narrow Chinese streets, their doors breathing opium and garlic ... Bombay ... iron cages full of black women who smelt like bulls. Algiers ... the steps of the Casbah ... waiting for a pistol-shot. Rio ... Wherever there's a red light at a crossroads. Stand as you were then, painted with a spatula ... James Ensor. Stand in my way. If I wanted – and I don't want – to pull the veil away from your face, I wouldn't find anything behind it. I know. Tu viens, Cheri? Cigarette? Take one. Wag your tongue in the air as much as you like, I won't come with you. I don't want to go up that crooked staircase. For every staircase, I know which step's missing. I know which wall's on the point of falling. The bed with the broken leg, the damp towel on the rail, the spilt bowl of permanganate, reminding me of Titian's cherry-red. The crooked picture on the wall, *Brave Timokleia before Macedon*. Then how you'll take your shoes off, pushing one with the other, without bending down. And afterwards I'll look at the worn carpet, holding the newspaper in my hand, and hear the squish of the douche-bag between your legs. No, I won't come up. I'd come with you if you had what I've been looking for all these years ... sideways, crossways ... Stand outside the door. I'll pay you to stand motionless, silent, without breathing. That carved wood statue I adore. Don't! ... Just go a little over there, a hair's breadth ... enough for that human thread, with arms like Karsavina's legs, to pass. What did you say? ... You're scared of Riccardo? You're hungry? Lies. Symbols feel no fear ... no hunger ... You smell of fish. The one who was killed smelt the same ... I remember. In Kalamas ... Take you with me? You don't know what you're saying. I always have you with me. Morning, afternoon, when I'm sleeping, on watch, when the watch is over ... always with me ... You, and all the journeys, and the fish-market, and that great human heap that has its arse where its head should be, and that dark cathedral with no services ... Giorgione di Castelfranco ... I, who strip the models for you, the dwarf from Calabria ... Find me the green ... Give me the paint ... Clean the brushes ... Sandro Dato ... We walked to Florence together, before the Balts killed me ... George Peter Seurat. The three great sons of the palette. I searched twenty years to find Cezanne's secret. Dawn, midday, sunset. In Aix, Vallon des Lauriers, Estaque. Don't laugh. If you dare laugh, I'll smash your head with these pliers. Finally I found it in Kifissia, at midnight. On the way down to Strophyli. I touched his way of seeing. You're laughing ... Balls to you ... Gold dust in Magellan's beard. Deal the cards, tell my fortune, explain my dreams ... You know where the pistol-shot will come from, where the knife-blade will flash, where the lasso will come from that will snare my legs. Legs ... legs again ... Ah! Marinella's! In that little street, Juge de Palais, shameful places ... You could just see part of the old harbour, and the hill of St Mary's church. They were taking you for your first communion. From the Coutellerie, from St Victoret, from all the streets around, the girls ran out to admire you. A winter's afternoon. One of them put your hat straight, another your veil, and Mimi your ribbons. I remember your skinny little legs. Much later I found them again, in the same street: as thin as ever, stained and tortured by worthless experience, hanging from the police van, just as they'd thrown you in after Anatol had killed you. Anatol, with the sideburns and the face destroyed by punches. Marinella ... Women have four legs ... Eh? ... Count mine, too? No, women don't ... they don't have legs ...

You're raving ... you're sick ... you're afraid ... No. Sick people have scars, pain. I've seen sick people. I've spent the night outside leper colonies in the South, outside the trenches dug round fields full of people with cholera, lazarettos ... So tell me ... tell me about the people who look in the mirror and see the first mark between the eyes, the white spots in their mouths, the red ones on their chests ... That's enough ... Open your eyes. When you shut them you see inside yourself, and that's no good. When they're open you only see what's round you ... until there's a mark ... That port in Chile, with the nitre. The ice-cream cart. The old woman wearing dusty holed shoes, who told the old tale of the endless street. No ... leave that for another time, don't remember it now ... Throw that damned bottle out of the porthole, it's full of sins and memories. So, the little girl was holding the woman's skirt in one hand and the ice-cream cone in the other. A beautiful sky-blue day. Consuela, look me in the eyes ... you haven't any, just two red holes. But tell me, where does it come from, then, that joy that lights up your face and makes it shine? ... Hey, you with the cart. I'll buy all your ice-creams, and the cart, and you, and the whole square, and the town and its nitre, and all the world beyond the sea, and I'll lay it at her feet for her ball, her toy. If she's ever seen colours, and remembers them, I'd be sorry ...

"Give her the colours."

But she can't see ... Who spoke?

"Give her your eyes to see with. You can only give what's your own. What your eye can reach, you can caress, you can hear. What's beyond is foreign, you can't reach it. D'you hear me?"

Yes. I'd die at her feet, if she asked.

"I said 'Just give her your eyes.'"

But – Devil take it – I'm hearing things worse than if I'd taken cocaine ... I wish someone would come and throw a bucket of water over my head. I wish the sea would come in and soak me, and make that chirping cricket stop, it's splitting the plates of my head like a power drill. Where did it get in? I've searched every corner of the wireless cabin, the ceiling, the holes, the bookshelf. Did it come on with the ship's stores, hidden somewhere in the vegetables? Along with the scorpions in Colombo? ... We killed the scorpions, but that invisible creature, I can't find it, I can't catch it, but it's somewhere near me, next to me, above me, inside me ... To begin with I enjoyed it. Reminded me of summer nights. Hay-ricks, thyme and oregano, cut grass. Oxen sleeping in the byres. That was the first day. But now I know it could drive me mad. Fool ... if you're born mad you've nothing to fear. Ah, there she is ... the mad woman in the ruins of the old port ... Lily!

It was in Marseilles, just after the war. The whole right-hand side, from the Mairie up to the Fortress of St John, had been destroyed by the German bombardment. A few cocottes sitting with their legs crossed in the cafés on the Cannebière. They were all new, but they looked just like their mothers. That's when I realized I'd got old. As soon as it got dark I crept into the Coutellerie like a burglar. The ruins started a hundred metres further on. I found Pegli, wearing the same beret he'd had before the war; he sold drink from some hole in the wall.

"Where are all the girls?" I asked him.

"Look around you— they loaded them on waggons and turned them into soap in Germany— and good luck to whoever washes with it. There's not one of them left."

"Not one?"

He wiped the counter with a duster. "Just one left behind— better if she hadn't been."

"Who?"

"Lily."

"Tell me, where is she?"

"When it gets dark, go through the alley behind the Mairie and into the ruins. Don't worry, no-one goes there. You'll find her there, searching in the rubble."

"What for?"

"Oh, questions— are you stupid? She's mad, I tell you. Clear off now, I'm busy" – some black girls had come in – "And come and eat with me tomorrow ... you're still the same old shit, you haven't changed at all ... what a mess ... and watch she doesn't bite you."

Chagall: Cimetière

I tripped on the stones, slipped in the mud and fell once or twice. Now and then I'd stop and look around. If these stones could talk! What strength had fed this earth, since the time of the Phoenicians!

I could see the lights again, as they used to be— the bridge back in its place. Doors opening and closing. I could hear the scratched records, the hits of '29. Piver's *Pompeia* caressing me. The crick-crack of the bead curtains in the beer shops.

At a time like this, before the war ... I saw that cadet from the *Argonaut*, sixteen years old, wearing a cap from Trieste, holding his money in his hand so as not to lose it. Some woman pulled at him gently: "Leave your money somewhere safe" – she took out a fiver and put it away in a drawer – "and later when you want it you can give me a franc." He doesn't remember her name, only how he got cut. She was more upset than him; she did all she could to stop the bleeding. She took him as far as the corner of the street; "Drink a couple of pastis," she told him, "and don't worry: it happens to everybody."

I opened my eyes and saw the ruins. I tripped again, this time not on a stone.

"Qu'est ce que tu veux?"

"Toi."

"Va-t-en."

"Lily."

"Laisse-moi tranquille."

"Cinammon."

That's what the Greeks had called her, from the colour of her hair. Her legs were the coldest white I've ever seen.

She got up to go; I caught her hand. "Police! Police!" she shouted; I let her go.

"I met Prosper," I shouted after her, "In Noumea."

She stopped. I saw her eyes light up; she made an imploring gesture and came back to me.

"Dis moi vite. Where is he?"

"He came out of prison. He's got a shop. Kept asking about you, told me to come and find you."

"Did he get married?" Her voice trembled.

"Ba, he'll be coming, I tell you. Soon as he's got the papers. Tell me, Lily, how did this happen? Why did they knock it all down?"

She interrupted me: "Is he O.K.? Did he get old?"

"Just like you knew him."

"The chains had left marks on his hands. Do they hurt him?" – I remembered how those hands had beaten her, taken her money, pulled out her hair – "Has he still got his teeth? His hair?"

"Perfect health, I tell you."

"I don't believe you. Did he give you anything for me, to remember him by?"

I undid my shirt and unpinned a little medallion of the Virgin Mary from my vest – I'd sold its chain during the occupation – and gave it to her. She brought it up to her lips, then closed her hand. I stopped feeling ashamed for the lies I'd been telling her. She sat on a rock, I sat on another opposite her. Her legs shone in the darkness. For a long time we said nothing.

"Veux-tu faire l'amour avec moi?"

"... I want to ask you something."

"Whatever you like."

"How did all this happen? How did it get knocked down?"

"Well ... That night I was sleeping with a black guy. The megaphones woke us up; we were supposed to take a bit of bread and go down into the street. It was blockaded. Cannons at every corner; machine-guns and rifles. There were four thousand of us; total chaos. Women coming down unwashed, hair all over the place, wailing, getting mixed up with the customers and the queers. Two Spanish terrorists who'd been hiding blew their brains out rather than fall into the hands of the Gestapo. And one of our own people too. I saw the oldest madam, Melanie, throw her gold jewellery out in the street, then jump out after it, from the third floor. By the evening they'd sorted us out: some to go to Baumet, some to Frejus, some to the barracks, the rest to be shot. When everyone was gone they started the bombardment. Ten days. They left that block over there, because there were a couple of ancient palaces. And the bell-tower, and the Chateau du Roi René. It wasn't them so much, it was our people who put them up to it."

"And the women?"

"They sent them off to the barracks, different places. Some just died, from the terrible treatment. Not one came back."

"Katina? What happened to her?"

She started to tremble; "Bonsoir, Niko."

"Tell me about Katina ... I'll be going back to Noumea ..."

Her voice dropped. "Why d'you ask me? It wasn't my fault."

I gave her a cigarette; she hadn't smoked for some hours. I took her hands and stroked them. She started to cry. I begged her. She softened, and started:

"Katina ... you loved her ... I remember ... in the war she had her shop near here. I worked with her. She hid some Greeks they were looking for for political things. I was going with a German, and I used to tell all the secrets I found out in Katina's. One night – we'd just closed, I was leaving by the back door – Katina wouldn't let me go; she locked the door and dragged me into the kitchen. She was horribly drunk ... her black eyes ... her hair ... no wonder you loved her. She took me by the hair and threw me down on the flagstones. She picked up the meat-cleaver and waved it over my head ... Madonna Mia ... then she pulled me up and pushed me against the wall.

"We're going to have this out, baby," she says. "Like women, not like stool-pigeons."

"Leave me alone! Why are you doing this? What have I done?"

"You've pissed on us," she said. "They got Mathio this morning as soon as he went out of that door. You gave him away. Don't even bother to cross yourself, I'm going to slaughter you like a lamb and throw you in the sewers."

"Then someone banged on the door with a pistol-butt. We straightened up and the door opened. It was Hans, my boyfriend. He took me and we left. They got her the next day; she passed right by me, in handcuffs. She spat at me ... Nikola ..." – her voice had dropped so low it seemed to come from a hole in the ground – "Nikola ..." She picked up a stone and kissed it ... "By the ruins where I was born, where I was ruined, where'll I'll die ... I didn't betray Katina ... On Prosper's life ... It was someone else."

It started to drizzle. I got up. She had her head on her knees. I tried to help her up.

"No. I'll stay here. When will I see you again?"

"Oh ... when I come back. In a few months. Where shall I look for you?"

"Here. On this rock, exactly. Check. Opposite the bell-tower, Rue de la Prison. Don't you remember? Here where we are were the steps of Prosper's shop, where three men fell, one after the other, from the blade of his knife. But he was right. Tell him I'm waiting for him ... here. Bon Voyage, Nikolas. I'll be waiting."

I went back to Marseilles many times. I didn't look for her. They started to dig, to lay foundations. They found a temple of Apollo. Scaffolding, reinforcing rods, cement. When they'd used up the lime, the builders found a dead woman at the bottom of the pit. A woman who'd once had legs whiter than lime ...

Women. Fourteen years old. The ones who'll turn into the worst whores later, who'll roll in stinking sheets, do it in the streets, under bridges, in the stand-up brothels with the straps round their knees and the loops round their shoulders; in churches, in shrines. And the ones who won't: who aren't fourteen any more, who'll never go with men, who never think of adultery, deceit, betrayal, who'll never defile themselves. They're all saints; all blessed.

"Anthi," I said to you one night, "You must have been blessed ... have you noticed a short, ragged, middle-aged nut-vendor who stares up at your window from dawn to dusk?"

"Yes. Been there a year or more. What's he after?"

"He wants you to like him. Call him up to your room one night."

"You're crazy. What would he want from me?"

"Your virtue."

"You're disgusting. I've always tried never to do anything I don't fancy. He'll stink ..."

"So much the better."

I expected her to be angry. I saw her frown thoughtfully. I was ashamed. I never saw the man again; I never went to her house again.

Anthi ... That's how it has to be. And we call *them* virtuous, who're not afraid of death.

Suppose a woman was baptized in fish-oil. Painted with anti-fouling below the water-line. Caulked with tar, her saliva salt water, her hair seaweed, her arms tentacles, her eyes the colour of the sea. Her legs ... no, no legs. Like the one in the aquarium in ... no. Nowhere. Only in my dreams. Call her 'Thalassini'; she talks the same language as the fish.

The engine's stopped. Heap of oil iron ... to collide ... to fall into the sea ... do we take ships, or do ships take us? They call ships "Irons" ... there are ships with male names, but they're just upside-down females. And there are some that hate you from the moment you first board them, they chase you off, they push you. You trip on the steam-pipes and scuppers. And there are others that want you, that make you their rivet, their bolt, their thole-pin.

The ensign staff. The iron. Good luck to them! Save a bit of money, give them the five fingers for ever. Don't go down to the sea, don't remember ... But who has seen more open wounds than those from rusty ship's plates, from rotten anti-fouling? Who has heard a more human sound than a ship's whistle, butting through the fog, or the moan she makes in a storm, even when no-one's pulled the whistle-wire? When she moans by herself, making love with the wind ...

Two eyes. Emerald green the one, ruby red the other. They call them navigation lights; they're eyes. We don't take ships; they take us.

Anonymous: Self-portrait.
To my sister Jenia.

Dizziness. Like in childhood, when the sea turned on me. What a vile thing, sea-sickness ... throwing up, bile. Turns you into a rag, a joke. You can't think of anything but getting off at the first port. And when you're there ... you forget it all and set off again. You start to get used to it, or so you think. The rolling doesn't bother you any more, but the pitching turns you over. Then that goes too. Now all you have to get over is when it rolls and pitches at the same time. Now you're fine. Then you change ship, and you have to learn new movements; every ship has its own. A cargo-ship sailor gets sick on a mail ship. Strange sickness. Medicine?— dry land. The deaf, and those who've lost their sense of smell, don't get sea-sick. Nor the mad.

I remember someone from the mountains who'd never seen the sea; he was crossing it for the first time. Volos to Kavala. Snow and strong winds. Everyone on the *Cassandra* like wet rags, all vomiting snakes. This peasant opens his bag and starts seasoning a chicken.

"Don't you feel ill, Barbar?" I say to him.

"What d'you mean?"

"Well, the way we're rolling. Doesn't it bother you?"

"The mule rolls too," he said.

I made a bet with the purser that I'd get the old man sea-sick, but the rougher the sea, the more he ate.

"Tell me, old man, is the sea rocking the mountain?"

For a while he looked first at the land, then at the sea. Finally he threw up.

"There, it's made you dizzy!"

"Who spoke? I'm frightened. That's a voice I know, I remember it, I've heard it before. But it doesn't belong to any of these sailors I'm travelling with."

"So who was it?"

"Well. You, who can make the passengers throw up if you want to, who've been twenty years at sea, who've crossed the line twenty times both ways, tell me: which side of your body d'you sleep on?"

"Half the night on the right, and the other half on the left."

"And in rough seas?"

"On my back."

"All right— you've confessed it affects you. And now tell me the story of Marie Laure."

"Who are you? I can't see you—"

"Doesn't matter. Tell me."

"Let me sit down."

"No. And don't lean on me, you'll dirty me. Speak."

"Marie Laure— I can't remember, it's gone— I want to go, I'm sleepy."

"You can sleep in port for twelve days. Speak."

"Not tonight."

"I'm listening."

"I can't remember."

"Speak."

"Yes ... wait ... you mean the young French girl in Bandol. Blonde, didn't use make-up, didn't play roulette, just lay on the verandah of the cheap hotel. Well ... what about her? ... I don't know ... I never saw her again ... Don't shove me like that ... I didn't love her, I swear it on the seas I travel, I don't ... only the sea ..."

"You don't even love your own body. You— you say 'I' and it fills your mouth. You travel because you're afraid of the land. You go with whores because you're a coward. Your need conquers your disgust. You're covered in tattoos. Pointless— you didn't get them done for your love of the sea— everyone gets tattooed when they're drunk, then regrets it, but you went sober. You just wanted something to show people. Show-off, always ready to turn cartwheels and make people laugh. You're poorer than a ..."

"Shut up. That's enough. I'll tell you about Gretchita, about Orayia, about ..."

"Marie Laure!"

"Give me my handkerchief."

"Take it."

"Give me the bottle."

"It's broken. When you've done I'll give you a glass; a looking-glass."

"Well then give me a cigarette."

"They've burst from the damp, the tobacco's spilt out."

"Fine. Listen then: I remember only her eyes: aquamarine. The most innocent eyes I've ever had the privilege of seeing. That winter I was looking after a cutter in Bandol. She told me she'd been working in a circus since she was seven years old, that she'd put her legs out and couldn't get up on the wire any more. She worked for three months every year in cabarets out east. Tiny creature, about twenty years old. Yes, I loved her; I asked her to marry me. She gave a strange laugh and said 'I would, but someone'd turn up one day and you'd realize you'd been made a fool of.'

"'I won't ask you anything about the past. Even if you've worked in the houses, it doesn't bother me.'

"She gave me a frightened look. 'It's something worse, a thousand times worse. I can't tell you.'

"I tried to convince her that nothing would shock me. Late that night I went with her to her place in the back streets. We got as far as the bed, and suddenly she got up and pushed me away: 'Go away! I don't want to see you any more! Get lost!'

"Well I knew, I'd heard, that most women do that at such moments, but if you draw back they're disgusted with you: call you a fool and give you the five fingers. I dragged her to the bed. She pulled a pistol out from under the pillow, as if it had been a Saint Vasili's day present hidden there: 'I'll give you all six!'

"Well I didn't know anything about pistols. I wasn't scared of the gun, it was her eyes frightened me. 'Just a word,' I said, 'Let me talk to you.' I held her tight, and she relaxed. Then I heard a bang and a bullet whistled past my ear and buried itself in the wall; with her other hand she was pointing at the door. Her breasts were all uncovered. I went out, but stopped at the top of the stairs; there was a ray of light spilling from the crack of her door. I heard her voice, low, pained: 'Good luck ... God bless you.' Then she closed the door, carefully. How many doors ... That's enough for you. I can't tell the rest."

"I want the whole story."

"Then lift me up and take me to the door a minute, for some fresh air."

Dawn had broken; the fog was clearing. Everything dripping. The stars had gone; just one still twinkling: it touched the tip of the mast, then faded. To port; the coast of China.

"Well you asked for it, so don't blame me. In five years I'd forgotten her. I mean completely; less than the itch of an old knife-wound in wet weather. Not even her name.

"A year before the war, we were unloading timber in Mex. The first evening my old friend Hassan turned up with his little carriage. 'Where shall we go, boss?'

" 'To the stables.'

" 'Shame on you. Won't do it. Let's go to Mavrouka, there's some good ...'

" 'To the stables, Hassan.'

"We set off towards the Mahmoudia canal.

"In those days the stables was the most expensive show in Alexandria; a pound. It's not there any more. We arrived; a stink of manure. The carriage waited a little way off. I gave the sign and they let me in. Two or three old tourist women, a young girl with freckles on her cheeks, a couple of foreign sailors in uniform, all standing up. In the middle of the stable was a dance-floor with a fence round it. A black guy in a filthy jellaba was selling photographs, and cigarettes with hashish in them. Another was collecting the pounds. Two more led on a skinny Nile donkey, caught in the month of August, and left it in the middle of the dance-floor. A woman jumped gracefully in over the fence, wearing a black kimono embroidered with red birds; it was open from top to bottom ... I can't go on. Come back tomorrow and I'll tell you the rest."

"Go on, dirty mate."

"Then she stood in front of the beast and started caressing its head ... it was Marie Laure ..."

"The old ladies watched every detail carefully, through opera-glasses. The girl put her hands over her eyes and drew back, screaming. The two sailors were laughing.

"'Hey!' One of the black guys shouted at me, 'Don't throw your cigarette down, you'll set fire to the straw!'

"A little bell rang sweetly— 'Hassan, follow that carriage and don't lose it. You'll get double baksheesh.' The whip cracked and we went into the back streets. We passed the 'Kinena' and the women rolled their bellies at us and shouted 'Wahat Selin'. We saw the lights of Ramleh, and finally stopped at a place on the Corniche. Hassan didn't want to go; 'Boss, you're sick ... no, no money ... I wait for you till tomorrow.'

"She was sitting on a bar stool with her back to me. In half an hour she drank five whiskies, without soda. I did the same. I made a sign to the waiter; he smiled ironically: 'Wait till I'm off and I'll take you somewhere better.'

"'It's her I want.'

"'Listen, my countryman— Aren't you disgusted?'

"'Can you do it? If not ...'

"'Fine. Wait.'

"He brought her to the carriage. We went to her room in the 'Sporting'. When we were face to face, I repeated a line she'd once told me disgusted her: '"J'ai une pitié immense pour les coutures de son ventre."' – Marie Laure ... Remember the pistol-shot in Bandol?'

"I watched her eyes – aquamarine – grow big, turn to seas I could drown in. Hassan was still waiting outside.

"'Babour,' she said.

"'Iwa.'

"Afterwards I found she'd hanged herself with her stockings two months later, in a cheap hotel in Bandol."

"And you? Why didn't *you* hang yourself?"

"Me? I was hanged that night from the rotten beams of the stable. They still haven't cut me down."

"You're a murderer."

"No. That's another story ..."

"You disgust me ... I'm going, you stink."

"Now, you'll stay as long as I want you to. I've got another story. No love, no sense, no justice. I want to see you throw up when there's no storm."

"No. I don't want to know. I'm sorry for you. I'm going."

"Do what the devil you like. Go, don't go, I'm going to get it off my chest."

The *Cafard* – Three hundred tons – We'd set out from Marseilles and follow the coast of Africa. We'd get through the straits of Gibraltar without being checked, and reach Casablanca. What a ship. The only thing missing was wheels on the sides. Fuel-tanks water-contaminated. We never got rid of the vermin. At night the rats sang like canaries; the size of cats. An Algerian stoker lost his nose while he was sleeping, a Frenchman his ear and a Maltese his balls. You know how they nibble? Gently. You don't feel it. Once we threw a cat in the hold; we never saw her again. You had to sleep with a pistol under your pillow. Not for the rats, for the person in the next bunk. Food? Boiled pasta and ship's biscuit. But we did all right; plenty of money. Every two months we'd hole up in Marseilles for a week. I had a girlfriend, Gaby, and I saved my money. She lived in an attic in the back streets. Beautiful girl, but rotten to the core. A liar and a thief. One night – we were leaving at dawn for Algeria – instead of waking me up at four as I'd told her, she got me up two hours earlier.

Winter. While I was getting dressed her tongue wouldn't stop: "Bring me – don't forget, write it down –" She stood in the doorway with her arms folded – there was no electricity in the house – and before I'd got four or five steps down she shut the door and I was left in darkness. I felt for my matches, but I'd forgotten them. Up again, or down? – I felt for the wall and started to go down cautiously. Dark as the grave, and a smell of mould – my eyes started to get used to the darkness. Three pistol shots, one after the other, right next to me, then two more from below. Someone fell on me, grabbed me, then fell and started to roll down the stairs. A door opened and someone came running out.

I was stuck with my back against another door. My hand found a cold doorknob. I turned it carefully, noiselessly. Two steps backward.

I was in the room and had closed the door. I ran my hands down from my head to my feet. I was wet in lots of places; something thick: my hands were sticky. I brought them close to my eyes, my nose, but without touching.

The room smelt of medicine. I coughed without meaning to. I heard a low whistle once or twice, then nothing. A strip of light fell across my eyes; I shut them quickly and staggered back and forth, as if drunk. The torch beam travelled round, came back again and stopped just to the right of me. I opened my eyes and looked. A disembodied white hand beckoned. "Please – lower the light a little so I can come," I whispered.

A hiss like a cobra's answered me.

The torch beam was lowered, just enough light for me to creep forward towards a bed. The covers were pulled aside, and I fell, still with my clothes and shoes on, next to a warm body. The light went out. I searched my pockets for a cigarette, but felt a hand restraining me.

Suddenly I heard noises in the street. Motorcycles, whistles, barking. There were sounds coming closer, up the stairs. The hand pulled the covers over my head and wrapped me up. A warm smell caressed me. A woman's body – it chases your fear away, calms you down, protects you. Next to one, on top of one, you forget that some day you'll be giving up the ghost. She stroked my forehead. I heard them open the door without knocking – "Permettez – Police –"

How many of them were there? I listened to their heavy footsteps, the cupboard opening; they searched under the bed.

"Excusez, mon enfant –" And, as the door was closing, "Pauvre Calamité!"

I heard their steps on the floor above, and Gaby swearing. I uncovered my head and looked for my Gauloises. She stopped me again, as if she were angry. I felt her soft hand caress me, but she wouldn't let me kiss her, and as we moved about I heard that hissing, continually. It gave me goose-flesh. I managed to kiss her. An empty, incomplete kiss, that seemed to try and slip away. There was a din again, in the house, in the street.

What was the time? How long had I got? The *Cafard* would be weighing anchor. A moment, just a minute – I'd get to the bottom of that hissing, and I'd leave. I stroked her emaciated face. A small nose. Thin lips, a tiny chin. Her throat – my hand stopped on something smooth, cold, metal, like a ring. I covered it with my thumb, held it closed. I felt her body tremble, shake – We'd be setting sail at dawn! I kissed her forehead. It was cold.

I went down the dark twisting stairs with my mind empty – Murder – Police – Fairy tales. I was gently rubbing my thumb against my forefinger.

The street deserted. I picked up a still-burning cigarette-end and took a drag. A clock struck six. Without hurrying, without looking, I found my way, street by street. A woman I'd seen around six the evening before, dressed up like a bride in all that cold, half-starved but painted, looked at me but hadn't the nerve to beckon me over. At the next corner a window opened and a bowl of water emptied over me. Porto Vecchio. Opposite, St. Victor's Abbey. The bridge – I'd come out too far to the left. Someone in uniform ran past me, dropped something shiny, turned at the fortress of St. John and stopped on the jetty. Just then, on the other side, the bugle sounded from the legion barracks. The man in uniform jumped into the sea. He'd make it in ten strokes; the barracks gate would stay open five minutes. He only had four or five yards to go. I thought of jumping for it myself. A launch full of police cut off the soldier's route. I turned away. I heard a bitter laugh nearby. I set off again at a run; I could see the smoke from the stack of the *Cafard*. A hundred yards – fifty – twenty – I got up the ladder. Miguel, the bosun, gave me a shove and I fell onto some coils of rope. Someone threw a bucket of cold water over me. I felt as if I were drowning in the Hudson river, at dawn, among the bobbing used contraceptives.

Where, on what bedside table, did you forget the medallion your mother pinned on your vest the morning you set off on your first voyage ... trees, gardens, mountains. Fresh water running, ferns, beds that don't rock, women who don't paint themselves, men who don't blaspheme. Whitewashed rooms in the country, without rivets on the ceiling. To get away for a while from all those things you've got used to and find, just before you go to sleep, those other things— to touch them, to smell them, to look at them as you close your eyes.

Beatrice d'Este ... I wonder about your first night, when you found yourself alone with that iron-bound man who'd come back from the battle, stinking of horses, wine and war. How can girls who've just got married sleep for the first time with a man they don't know, whose breath they've never smelt ... how could my mother ... it's something that brings my guts to my mouth ... Beatrice ... and next to you, I'll put out the portrait of the little Florentine, because it suits you. I can see it in your eyes. His hands ... the whole portrait's built around his hands, one hanging with a twisted finger and the other half-hidden, just four fingers resting on the sleeve ... "Andrea Foscari, mignon du Cardinal de Raguse" ...

When I came to we were off Planier. The Captain used his worst curses on me for the delay. I've never had a worse journey; we called at Algiers, Tunis, Moustaganem, Oran, Tangier, Rabat, and Casablanca, but I didn't go ashore at any of them; I bought what I needed from the bum-boats. Every time we hit harbour I expected the police to come for me. What was I afraid of? I don't know. In Tangier I decided to jump ship; I changed my mind at the last moment.

And one spring morning we saw the spire of Notre Dame de la Garde breaking through the mist ... I felt like walking to it barefoot to pray ... deliver me from evil ... we were free. It was after five, and people were putting on their best clothes and leaving one by one. I sat outside the galley and thought about it. No-one came to look for me; would they get me on shore? Should I go, or not? The Algerian cook, a drunkard and hashish-smoker, who used to go to the steward every day with an empty bottle, asking for wine for the stew – we never had that sort of food on the *Cafard* – came out wiping his poxy face with his filthy apron and said to me "I don't like the look of you, Greek boy. You must have done some dirty work if you're not going ashore." He blew his nose with his fingers and wiped them on the bulkhead. Rolled a cigarette, took a deep drag and passed it to me: "Not even a bridegroom gets to smoke this stuff; I just cooked it." Greedily I took a drag, then another. He pulled it out of my mouth, cursing: "You've ruined it, you Casbah bastard."

Just then the Captain passed; he stopped beside me. He was a middle-aged Corsican, good sailor, better person. Never swore or blasphemed; we all respected him. What was he doing on this old wreck? "Come tomorrow morning," he said, "and I'll pay you off, you're being discharged. The ship's being held. I've got no argument with you, you're all the same dirty dogs. If you hear that we're off again, come and find me in the Café Samaritain."

There was still a little of that sweet light, that joy of Marseilles, separating dusk from night. Just as I was, in my dirty uniform, I jumped down onto the dock.

The customs guard didn't beckon me over, but I stopped and gave him a cigarette, struck up a conversation. What for? To play with fear. And if he'd searched me? I was swaddled in about ten metres of silk, with a couple of kilos tucked inside. And that's apart from what we'd be sharing out that night; my bit of the stuff stolen from the cargo.

I went up the steps of the cathedral and watched the customs guard, smoking, below me. Would they get me?— Ba— No work tomorrow. Never mind, I'd got enough to last me a couple of months.

It was dark by the time I reached the Place de Lanche. I could hear children playing. One little girl was apart from the others, crying. I'm a child myself; I took a chocolate from my pocket and gave it to her. She took it, looked at it a while, then threw it in the mud and cried all the louder. A poorly-dressed woman grabbed the child, spanked her bottom, then turned and cursed me in a drawling accent. It's a bad sign when the children don't want you and the adults chase you away. I stopped in front of a mirror outside a shop and looked at myself. I was shocked: tiredness and fear had given me a long face, my ears looked like little horns, there were dark circles round my eyes. My lips were swollen and bleeding from stuck cigarette-papers. A cloth cap and a stevedore's rags that had once been a sailor's clothes— the woman had been right.

Fear ... Once, at the customs in some port, the guard stopped some sailor: "What are you hiding on yourself?"

"But— two thousand dollars, maybe a bit more, I didn't have time to count it all."

He looked at him with contempt, gave him a shove: "Yes, I can tell from your eyes. To the devil with you, idiot!"

A little Indian customs post. A sailor looks about, then grabs the controller's rubber stamp while he's talking to some passengers and stamps a case full of drink and perfume – enormous duty, or two years inside. He goes towards the exit, shaking a little. The guard in his yellow turban smiles at him, looks at the stamp and pats him on the back.

Another time, another sailor: outside the fence at some harbour, waiting for someone to come and collect twenty-five gold lires. The ship's whistle blew insistently three times; he thought of dumping the gold through the sewer grating. He blinked and looked round: A little way off a fellahin was selling broad beans. He went and took a piece of his old newspaper, made it into a cone, put the money in, then another bit of crumpled paper to hide it and said "Give me some."

The cone was full to the top; he had to hold it with both hands. The guard searched him from head to foot, then took a few beans. A little further on a plain-clothes guard checked him; he took a handful too. There was the ship— the sailors had just raised the gangplank. The guards at the bottom searched him and shoved their hands greedily into the cone; a bit deeper and they'd have been pulling out lires. The lieutenant called to them in their own language "That's enough, leave him alone." He saw the rope-ladder being rolled down and stopped dead: a rope-ladder needed two hands. Drop the gold in the sea? "Hurry up, then," they shouted from above. Quickly he crumpled up the paper, which was starting to fall to bits, and stuffed it into his clothes. He was wearing overalls too big for him, with a bit of string round the waist. He went up, everybody staring at him from above. Jumped onto the deck, the coins ringing merrily. Nobody noticed; they were all looking at his eyes.

Strange thing, but all those sailors had the same eyes: empty, washed out. Always sleepy. And they say fear can't be hidden.

To Nikos Fameliaris.

The Rue de la Loge in all its glory, the girls walking up and down. Not one of them called to me. I went into the Chinaman's shop and did the business; we came to an agreement. I left him the hashish, he filled my pockets with money. And now— Gaby— But how could I go up those stairs again? ... I remembered those damp hands, that whistling. Again, I found myself rubbing my thumb and forefinger together. Like a sleepwalker, I found myself outside the house. Tired out, I went and sat in the bar opposite. I wasn't hungry; I didn't feel like a drink, or a woman. I just wanted to know. To loosen the ties of fear. Titin the waiter brought me a pastis without my asking. His feet stank unbearably. I didn't take my eyes off the house opposite. The street was buzzing; she must come down. Time for business. Unless she'd gone into a brothel, stopped working the streets. Or died. If she doesn't come down in five minutes I'll have to go and see.

An Indochinaman came out buttoning his trousers. An ageing cocotte, a queer patting his hair, then a dwarf, an old woman, a sailor.

A woman took my pastis and drank it, then lit a cigarette from my packet: "Can I sit here?"

"No."

"You're rough. Are you waiting for someone?"

"Yes. D'you know Gaby?"

She laughed sarcastically; "Mon enfant, there's a Gaby on every corner. Me too, I'm called Gaby. Alors, tu viens?"

I gave her a franc and she left. Somewhere a clock struck nine. No-one was looking at me, but I felt as if everyone was. I left. I was two metres from the door of the house. I was like an acrobat who's lost his balance; I felt as if I was on a caïque ... Devil take it, that's my secret: no-one knows, not even my mother. I can never board a caïque. That plank, from the jetty to the gunwale, I've never been able to cross it. Why? The worst that could happen would be to fall in the sea. I know how to swim. But always I just stand there, full of fear. If someone on the caïque were to hold one end of a thread, and me the other, I could cross a gangplank two hundred metres long. If I were to let go of the thread, I'd fall for sure. And at that moment I felt as if I was half-way across a gangplank without a thread. I hesitated a moment to get my balance; someone in a hurry bumped into me and I found myself inside. I went up to the first floor. The second. The third. There I was, right by the door. It opened and someone came out; I expected him to trip over me and fall over. He went down the stairs two at a time, whistling. There was a light on the stairs now. I knocked on Gaby's door. She came after a few moments, wearing nothing but a pair of black stockings.

"Cheri Niko! Come back in quarter of an hour, I've got a customer— what have you brought me?"

"A ring."

"Give it to me and go away."

I waited outside the door. After ten minutes I went in.

"Sit down. Wait while I wash."

She went behind the screen; I heard water running. She came and sat on my knees. She was wearing the ring with the green stone; I forced myself to endure her caresses. 'You can stay with me all night,' she said, "Only go and do some shopping, I haven't got a thing. Off you go; don't be long."

"Listen, Gaby, I haven't slept for two nights. I haven't the strength to go up and down the stairs. Take that and do the shopping yourself."

She put on a tatty dress and went out. I was on my own, looking at the yellowed photographs and the artificial flowers. A saucepan was bubbling on the Primus stove, the lid going up and down rhythmically. I took it off the flame. Hanging on the wall, the eternal clyster, its pipe swinging against the engraving of the Corsican in his three-cornered hat. Below it, the bidet. Fortunately it was spring and there were no grapes; the summer before we'd had tons of grapes. She used to block the hole of the bidet, fill it with ice and we'd put the grapes on top. As the ice melted we'd eat the grapes cold. I went to the window, that looked over ruined roof-tops. Samra's wooden leg was leaning in a corner of the room: I'd often wondered what had become of it. On the ship I used to help him stuff it with Camels – held a hundred and fifty packets. Once we got four kilos of coke in it with no trouble. By now he'd have a new one. Gaby had worked for a long time so they could order a lighter one from Paris, to hold more. They never searched Samra in the customs. He'd lost his leg at Ypres; he wore a rosette on his chest.

Gaby came back with her arms full: "I got scorpion-fish for soup. Go out for a walk while I cook it."

I didn't want to; I lay on the bed with my shoes on. At my feet, spread out, the faded cloth you find in every whorehouse in the world. I watched her take the saucepan to the wash-basin and tip out some boiled cloths. She filled it with water and put the fish in. When she'd finished she came and lay down beside me.

"It's beautiful, the ring you brought me. Is it gold?"

"Yes."

"What else did you bring me?"

"A scarf."

"Where is it?"

"I've got it tied round my waist."

"Take it off, quickly! It'll be like a lamp-wick!", and she started to pull my trousers off with greedy hands. "Cochon. What are all these safety-pins? Ah! What lovely silk! Is it for me?"

"No, someone ordered it."

"Mon loup. But take it off, I'll look after it for you."

"Leave it alone. They're expecting it tonight."

"But— aren't you staying with me?"

"I'll go out and come back."

"Mon vieux ... when are you off again?"

"Don't know ... I'll stay about two months."

"Magnifique! You can sleep here at night, for nothing. I mean, not much ... why don't you say anything? Tapette!"

"I want ... see ... a room of my own. Near ... on the floor underneath ... yes, so we can be near. If ... the one under this one, on the right as you go down."

"Don't be stupid— it's rented."

"Since a long time?"

"Yes, since they found Calamité dead— no, killed. So, you'll stay with me. In the summer we'll go to Cassis."

"Calamité? Who ..."

100

"Pakita, mon maquereau. A teacher. So, how much did you make?"

"Oh, about seven thousand ... And how did they find her, this ..."

"I'll tell you— Seven thousand! That's a lot— I'll look after it for you, I've got a metal box – you can keep the key. Kiss me ... how you've changed ... you're cold."

"Look, about the room— can you ask? It'll only take a minute."

"Oh! you're killing me. Even if it was empty I wouldn't let you take it. It was a sick woman who lived there. She died while you were away."

"How?"

"There was a murder that night, on the floor underneath. They killed a Brazilian bosun. The woman he slept with, it was her fault. That's what happens when you go with women you don't know. You, you're careful, but you don't always know. Anyway the murderer had the nerve to go into Pakita's room afterwards, to hide I suppose. They didn't find her injured, but there were marks on her body and the sheets. Blood. Seems the bastard tried to steal the platinum; it would make me sick."

"What platinum?"

"Pakita had a hole in her throat, to breathe. They'd put in a cannula."

"What did she have?"

"They didn't find out. Cancer, tuberculosis ..."

"Syphilis, maybe?"

"Oh ... she wasn't like us. She was a good girl, decent. The animal raped her before he left, the doctor said."

"Did they catch him?"

"No. Either he managed to get into the Legion, or else he got away in a ship."

"Was she beautiful?"

"Ba— like a tapeworm. Blonde. Nice girl. But come on, kiss me, why are you sitting there like a fool?"

"Gaby ... tell me, is my voice hoarse?"

"Yes. Who knows what you've been smoking and drinking on your journeys?"

I got up; "I'll be back in a quarter of an hour."

"Fine. But leave your money here; this time of night it's dangerous."

"I'm going to get paid now."

"Shall I come too? See you don't get cheated?"

"No, wouldn't do. But shine a lamp so I can get down the stairs."

"A lamp? Are you drunk or crazy? I think you must be sick." She turned the switch and there was light on the stairs. "Don't be long, ma tapette."

I stopped outside Calamité's room. To hold the handle – just for a moment – just to touch it. Which hand? Both, then. Someone will come out. Someone else is coming up.

I left the street door half-open behind me. I didn't go back. I didn't see Gaby again. But often, even in summer, my fingertips get cold, and I can't touch anything metal. Not even gold.

Cocky the parrot climbed onto the roof of the wireless cabin, folded his moulting wings and shouted "Merde, Signor del Mundo."

Marmaro the monkey stopped stuffing his greedy mouth to say "Old barge! they never tie you up."

A snake glided up to them. Cocky backed off; he took hold of the aerial down-lead in his beak and climbed up high. The monkey sidled up to the snake and asked him "Where did you get aboard?"

The snake hissed "Sabang."

"D'you bite?"

"No. A magician pulled my teeth out."

"How did you get here?"

"In a crate of vegetables."

"How?"

"I was asleep, I didn't mean to come. What is this place, a prison?"

"A ship."

Suddenly a cricket started up. "Rattle," said the monkey; "If it weren't for you we'd have gone mad. D'you remember ..."

"Land! Land!" Cocky interrupted.

"Malaka," muttered the monkey, 'I've known that since yesterday. And you think you're something because the Portuguese goes about with you on his shoulder."

"Rospou! Kachpe! Kaltak! Land!"

"And what are you going to do about it? You're free, but you don't go. I'm off as soon as we hit shore."

"How did they catch you?" asked the snake.

"In a trap, two years ago."

"And how's it going?"

"Not so good— yesterday some sailor made the five fingers at me. Why?"

Polychronis, don't let it drive you mad.

"Querotiro ... Puta quetaparios."

"Shut up!"

"What's that moaning?" asked the snake.

"Ah— there's a human under us."

"Is he dying?"

"No— he's drunk."

"Drunk?"

"Alcohol. One day they put some in my water. You dance, you yell, then you sleep."

"Tobacco! Cigars!"

He's a tough one, Cocky – he smokes, he won't pass over a dog-end. And he tells tales; that's why they love him here on board.

"Omak! Abouk!"

A rumbling, then the clouds seemed to lower. A big bird landed in front of them, its wings open.

"Welcome, you piece of shit," said Cocky.

"You found the right place," said the monkey.

"I'm a crow ... I'm lost."

The snake cleared off quickly.

"Where are you from?"

"The mainland."

"How d'you get here?"

"I was on my way to the islands."

"Migrating?"

"What's that?— I just left. They injured me, there's a war on out there."

"Are there coconuts?" – Cocky was climbing down – "Mangoes, Pineapples? I've decided to leave."

"If you eat dead bodies you'll like it there. You'll get fed up with eating them. They're the cleanest food: there's poison in the water, in the grapes, in the rice, in the trees."

"Who put it there?"

"The whites."

"Who are they fighting?"

"The yellows."

"Why?"

"Who knows! Happens a lot, they say. The place isn't big enough for them."

"But they're dying ..."

"And being born."

"Why don't they cut their balls off?"

"That's what they live for." The big bird spread its wings, took off and landed on the mast, forward of the wireless cabin ... Dawn broke.

The sun. A ray falls across his face. He waves it away. Another ray from the porthole makes patterns on his face. His voice has gone; only his lips play.

"Why didn't you go?"

"Shut up you crook ... fucken mate ... the knife and the rope. Rottenness and sickness. You feed on their breath. You get fat and live ... I spit on you."

"And I can't be bothered to wipe it off. Who are you?"

"'From out of the depths.' Remember that half-torn book you found in a second-hand bookshop in Assos? Full of engravings? 'Ben Braes and Little Will'; 'The Baobab Tree'; 'King Digo Bigo' ... We parted one night, many years ago, on the jetty in Pireaus, behind the ship's sterns. You heaved up your kit-bag, and left me behind with a book in my hand. I was afraid to come with you."

"Yes ... now I remember you. You wore a straw coolie hat with a narrow band ... in Fiskardo ... you used to fish with a little bamboo stick. You only caught tiddlers. You never learnt to swim like your brothers. You set lime twigs, but never caught a blackbird or a goldfinch, just a cuckoo. The whole village laughed. The other boys went after the girls who were there for the summer. I took you by the hand up the ruined staircase in Vasiliki's place – Vasiliki from Lefkada. The mattress smelt of milk and dirty washing ... we didn't part. You left me. Coward ..."

"That's enough."

No voice left; his lips shape the word: "Help ..."

Part 3

Anonimo XIV sec: Trionfo della Morte

To Eva Deli

Take me by the hand and show me the world. The great torn map, geography lost among useless books. No lenses in the sextant: they took them out to light cigarettes. The dividers broken, parallel rulers false. The compass needle wandering, mad. The tender's line's been cut by a big fish, perhaps a shark. The hour-glass? The sand can't struggle through. Let's measure the sun with our fingers ... which of the suns?

"A bit of ship's biscuit ..."

"Take some ... Why are you spitting?"

"Water."

"It's finished."

"You said you'd open a vein for me."

"Look! I did; not a drop runs out."

"Look! Land! Three palm trees!"

"No, five ... seven ... a thousand ... thousands. Near; not half a mile."

"Give me the oars."

"They're completely rotten."

"Then we'll swim ashore."

"Look at the shark's mouth, waiting for us."

"Throw him the ship's biscuits."

"He sicks them up and throws them back at us, don't you see? Wait, I'll jump. He'll eat his fill and you'll get to land. It's blowing: an off-shore wind; we're moving away. It's raining. Drink. Go to sleep; I'll watch over you."

"I'm asleep; I've been asleep a long time."

"How beautiful your hair is. Let me comb out the salt."

"No."

"Why do you slide out of my arms? Where are you? I've got a new tattoo to show you. Don't wake up ... as you are now, I'd make you a figurehead, on the bow ... little girl, take me by the hand and show me the world."

"I have no hand. There is no world."

Two men gone! You remember them? One drowned, as soon as he'd made Captain. Off Sigri. The sea sicked up his shoes, size forty-five. What fish is swimming with his ring? The next day the sea knew nothing of it, shone like a lake in the winter sun. At night it was smashing the ship's plates, by morning it had had enough. Its surface decorated with just a few patches of oil, two or three barrels, and broken timbers. A copper coffee-pot sailed by on a piece of cork. Eighteen; a good haul. No-one on the surface. A white life-buoy, decorated with twine, bumps against a box. The life-buoy the mail-ship passengers put one foot on, to be photographed. We are few who know that it's more than an ornament. Carefully painted with black letters: "Hope of Piraeus". The ferry-boat searched the area till night, gathered up the remains to take to the coastguard. They'll cross her off the register, and write in red ink: "Lost with all hands off the North-West coast of Mytilene, 20th of January 1939." That's all.

The other? ... Master of a cargo ship for twenty-nine years. Clear-eyed, quick, handled her well. The whole of seamanship at his fingers. Got stuck on a sandbank somewhere in the south, middle of the night, listing forty-five degrees to starboard. On the right course: he went to the chart-room when he saw she was stuck fast, and checked everything. No-one had got anything wrong. Mistake in the chart? He went to his cabin and killed himself, just as the First Mate came to knock at the door to tell him the ship had freed herself, unholed, and to ask him for a course.

A lone seaman came by in his boat – couldn't the mule have come by an hour earlier? – and explained the mystery to the First Mate.

Every six years the waters there flowed away, then came back three hours later before dawn. He laughed as he told it, flashing his white teeth. Every six years.

It wasn't written in any book. It never is.

They went out into deep water and sent him to the bottom. That's what happened to him.

And others ... thousands of others. A deep full of bones and uniforms. And there's a metal box, with letters, and something half-dissolved, in the shape of a hand. She who wrote the letters sleeps in a strange bed now, sighs under another's breath. Nothing troubles her sleep, not even the sea, as it comes from far off to beat on the threshold of her island house. If she's a mother, she nails her windows shut, paints them black outside, and never cooks fish. If she's a sister ... everyone stops crying sometime; only a mother carries on to the end.

The old ones don't cry. But there's a knot that comes up; a noose. It's what makes landsmen write books, and sailors carve and rig caïques in bottles; tattoo their bodies. When the books are good, the caïques masterpieces, the tattoos full colour, then ...

Inshore waters! All the kitchen sinks, all the night's foulnesses, all the shit-houses in the world, all drain to the sea.

And the shore's covered in sardine tins, hair-combings, chair-legs, holed shoes. Full of girls, swimming, enjoying the water. I give you the sea.

Coffee for the Pilot.

The sun rises higher. A small boat rocks on the water. In it, a naked sailor holds up two big fish in his hands, moves them up and down, and another cups his hands to call "Wota ... Wota ..." Water for fish. The *Pytheas* draws near them. Her derricks have been ready since early morning, the winches oiled, the cement broken in the hawse-pipes. The bosun's testing the gear in the bows. Captain Yerasimos, wearing a cap with a broken peak, stops outside the wireless officer's cabin. "Are you shaving?"

"Yes."

"You were in a state last night. Couldn't you have waited till we got ashore?"

"What d'you mean?"

"Oh come on! Are we children, or are you rehearsing the Chinese revolution? The steward found you flat on your back in the wireless cabin. Dead to the world. He came and woke me up, and we carried you to your cabin. My God, you know what a state you were in? Anyone else would have picked you up by the legs and thrown you in the sea."

"Why didn't you?"

"Feeling a bit touchy?"

"Ba ... Remember Nikita? They pulled him out of the mud with a grapnel, in the River Plate."

"Suicide?"

"Yes. He tied his hands and feet and jumped."

"What are you saying?"

"How he tied himself up by himself, with those knots, is another story. And it seems he hit his head with a lump of iron before he jumped."

"As he was falling?"

"No. Before he jumped."

"The devil he did. Such stories, in broad daylight. I don't remember him. How did it happen?"

"When they take women on the cargo ships, and they hang their underwear to dry in the rigging, on the rails, what d'you expect?"

"What are you talking about! We sailors are decent people; we keep our eyes lowered."

"Our women aren't. The salt and iodine upset them; they get their periods twice a month."

"Oh, rubbish!"

"I swear it on my eyes! The cleaners and washerwomen on the mail-ships told me. Another chap – wireless officer too – went up on the bridge, they gave him a coffee, and he went to meet his maker. You lot, you're all together; more than three perching on every branch. Me, I'm on my own."

"You can't take a joke today. Give up drinking again."

"Did you find a bottle on the floor?"

"No. Looks as if you swallowed that too. Look, do what you like, but let's not make fools of ourselves in front of the crew. Oh, yes, I nearly forgot: he found a big land bird, with a broken leg, by your head."

"What colour?"

"Blue, green and white, and flecked with blood."

"Did you kill it?"

"The bosun's got it. He put splints on its leg. He's called it Christopher, to remind him of Pharsa."

"When do we hit port?"

"We take the pilot on in three hours. We should be alongside by five."

"Bravo! We made good time."

"Good or bad, the point is we got here. Others set out and never get there."

"Yes. Look! It's a nice day! Everyone who got drowned yesterday will be changing their minds today."

"Stupidity … What are we going to do about the cadet? *I* can't go ashore … agents, insurance, stevedores, cuckolds. We can't just leave him, it's full-blown. Have *you* got the nerve to take him? He'll be infectious."

"Don't worry … if any of the thirty-three of them – how many are we? – tells you he hasn't got it, bring him to me so I can spit on him."

"You're exaggerating."

"And anyone who hasn't got it yet will get it tonight."

"Well, will you take him?"

"Yes, of course. Is the water on?"

"Since this morning. Go and have a bath, you'll feel better."

"We stink."

"What d'you expect? Nobody died from stinking, it's thirst that kills. Or you think I enjoy washing myself in a few inches of water in a bucket? Look, we'd better think about where you'll go …"

"Would it be O.K. to ask the quarantine doctor?"

"No."

"The pilot?"

"Nor him. A stevedore maybe, but even then carefully. You said you'd got a shore-leave guide; look it up."

"Hang on ... Sao Domingo ... Santos ... it's not there."

"Look under 'Sw'."

"Suva ... Swansea ... Ah, Swatow. Listen:

Seamen's Home	None.
Seamen's Agencies	None.
Hospitals	None.
Venereal Disease Physicians	None.
Dentists	Yes, Doctor Lin.

Well done, harbour! Pity it's not his teeth that're giving him trouble. Listen, this is a laugh:

Note: Nothing of interest to bring men ashore. Vicious conditions. Avoid riksaw men at night.

"Ha, ha ... that's all we need. Tell the boys to watch what they're catching. Listen, ask one of the Chinese in the office; I'll wait for you to tell me. Let's get it over with tonight. He asked me about it three times during the watch and he's been following me about like a dog since I got up. As soon as you're done, tell me what he's got. If I'm asleep, wake me up, and if the answer's 'yes', get whatever medicine the doctor says. Oh, and I meant to say, if it's O.K. with you, we'll pay for it ourselves fifty-fifty and sort it out later."

"Oh, yes. I was going to suggest it myself but you've beaten me to it. Ah! ... Shit in your trousers!"

"What's the matter?"

"Cut myself. Give me the cotton wool and the matches. On the shelf, to the right. Thanks. I'm scared of cuts."

"Let it bleed a bit, then press it hard. That's it ... why can't you get used to the razor? It's easy."

"The razor ... light and gentle ... you often think of it ..."

The bosun interrupted them: "We've untangled the cargo nets. Sounded the depth. O.K. I lifted the anchors a touch, to be ready. Any other orders?"

"Nothing. Have the lines ready. Fenders, rope-ladder."

"All done, all set up."

"That's it, then. We'll divide the watches as usual."

"Money? What shall I tell them?"

"Tomorrow afternoon. And the overtime, all together. And don't forget to tell them from me there's a war on out there, so they'd do well not to stay overnight in the brothels. Go around in groups, not alone. Don't drink the water, it's contaminated. Nor the alcohol, it's poison."

"So what'll they drink? Piss?"

"Their problem. How's the bird?"

"Gone. He was sitting as still as a corpse, then he made such a flapping I got scared. As for when he took off ... I'm going to go and eat."

"Did the bleeding stop?" asked Yerasimos.

"Yes. You'd make a good priest, Mema. In some village. Gathering round you on Sundays, bringing you offerings ..."

"Don't joke about it ... it'd be better than this job."

"Trouble is you'd forget yourself now and then and start blaspheming."

"The pimps on Omonia Square are better off than us. Reading the paper in bed, coffee beside them. Know what I thought during the watch? There's no hell for sailors in the next life, they go through it inside these iron walls, in this life. We're already forgiven, whatever we do, before they absolve us."

"D'you ever go to confession?"

"Yes. In my village."

"Me, never."

"Just as well. Your mouth's too polluted for confession, the places you put it ..."

"You blaspheme too."

"You think that's the same? ... Listen, here's a good one: yesterday that cuckold Spyros took his lighter to pieces up on the bridge. Dropped a screw and it fell in the sea. Know what he said?"

"How should I know?"

"He cursed the donkey that carried Christ into Jerusalem."

"The sod."

"Did you ever know Spyros Trizatos, from Pylaros?"

"No."

"My God, what sort of a bloke was that! You'd say 'Good morning' to him and he'd blaspheme. The Captain fined him a shilling for every blasphemy. 'I don't want to hear you blaspheme on my ship,' he told him. By the evening he owed a month's wages in fines. In the morning they couldn't find him, then they heard shouting and blaspheming coming from somewhere aft. They searched the deck; nowhere. Then they looked over the stern and what did they see? He was hanging on the painting-scaffold, outside the ship, sitting on a plank with his legs dangling over the propeller, smoking and blaspheming. Had his kit-bag hanging on a line beside him.

"'Idiot dog, what are you doing?' they shouted; 'You'll hang yourself.'

"'What am I doing, you donkeys? He- and she-devils enter you all! I've disembarked, and tell that goat of a Captain I'm blaspheming *off* his ship!'"

"Well me, if I lose something, I can't find it again unless I send it to the devil. But I don't use heavy blasphemies."

"It's better to blaspheme."

"What d'you mean?"

"Oh, it's a long story. Let's go and eat."

"I'm not hungry."

"I'm going."

> *In Hebrew his name was Abaddon,*
> *and in Greek Apollyon.*
> *(Apocalypse.)*

A double ring on the bell; twenty minutes to midday. In the fo'c'sle Linatseros was eating hurriedly at the stained, unpainted table. Polychronis was chewing a stalk of oregano and Yiakoumos the carpenter was mopping his tin plate with a scrap of bread. Four bunks against the bulkhead, and another two, one over the other, at the far end; all unmade. The sailor from the Black Sea was sitting on an upper bunk cutting his toe-nails.

"Well Kosma ... but leave your feet alone, it's making me sick."

"So, to cut a long story short, there in the Bario Cino, as I was saying, in Barcelona ..."

"Before the war?" interrupted Polychronis.

"Shut up, you lump of beef," said Linatseros. "You keep interrupting the man. It's a bad habit."

"Yes, before the war. I'd drunk a few bottles of Madeira. I picked up a girl in the back streets ... beautiful. Bit skinny. We came to an agreement ..."

"How much?" Polychronis interrupted.

"How should I remember? ... we went up ... fell on the bed ... What underwear! All silk and lace. 'You want it like woman,' she says, 'Or ...?' I didn't understand. I put my hand on her and felt stubble. Rough stubble."

"What?"

"It was a man, idiot, dressed like a woman. 'Maricon,' they call them. Well I get dressed to go and there's such a fuss it wakes the whole neighbourhood. 'You'll pay me for the full thing, you threw me on the bed, who said you could? ... You'll pay me!' Such squeaking and squawking! I was off; expect he's still cursing. I fetched him a few thumps ..."

Linatseros brightened and smiled; "We'll believe you if we want to, Kosmas. Last year in Cardiff you spent a week inside, when you were handing out sweets to the kids in Roath Park. And in Rotterdam, if you hadn't jumped on that tram as it passed, they'd still be beating you up. And in Denmark you filled the fo'c'sle with bloody kids ... giving them stamps! What d'you want me to remind you of next? ... Anything to be ashamed of in Barcelona? You can't patch your stories up nicely. They're tough as sail-cloth and the needle breaks."

"I don't deny it, Linatsa. But I'll tell you how it is with me: I could go with a woman who was wearing men's clothes, but I couldn't – how to put it – I just don't fancy going near a man in skirts. That's it, see?"

"Caïques are for fishing ..." Linatseros muttered.

"You think it's the same, when you see a fourteen-year-old in short trousers, his thighs all red from the woollen pants and the cold? We call them 'Tuna fish' where I come from. Think about it … Women stink …" and he spat.

The carpenter folded up his pocket-knife, gathered up the breadcrumbs and said, without looking at anyone, "Tell me, then, I'm confused: I read in a book that whoever's got the one vice has got the other one too."

"Must have read it in the lavatory," the Black Sea man interrupted.

"Oh, yes? And I've seen you hanging around outside the mosque to catch them."

The man from the Black Sea jumped up, red in the face.

"Calm down," said Linatseros quietly. "Tell it gently, Yiakoumos."

"Well … when you fry fish, how d'you put it in the pan?"

"First one side, then the other."

"Right. And there's a saying that a silk eiderdown is just as warm on top of you or under you."

Everyone laughed.

"I shit on you tar-arses," growled the Black Sea man. "I should have known you when you were younger, you Carthaginian buffaloes." He made the five fingers with both hands at the carpenter and left, swearing.

"He'll get over it," said Linatseros. "It's not the first time, or the second, he can't take it, the black sod. But he'll be the one to talk first. The Turk! The other day the bosun asked him why he doesn't get married … 'I'm waiting,' he says, 'for the Sultan to give permission for men to marry men.' And you, Rozos, why don't you get married? You're getting old; what are you waiting for?"

The carpenter spat on the floor and hit the table. "I've learnt not to take off my underwear without good reason. And I'm afraid of the cuckold's horns. Once we arrived at Argostoli at dawn, on the *Yperochi*. The cook had just killed some rams and he was throwing the horns in the sea. One of them fell in a rowing-boat. The boatman picked it up, looked at it carefully, and asked the chap in the next boat 'Hey, Louretzo, what's this here?' Suddenly a whole load more horns fell into the boat like rain, and this Louretzos cupped his hands and shouted 'It's nothing, Sigonto, nothing. Just the Captain and crew combing their hair.'"

"Heard it before. But since you were talking about underwear, the strangest I've ever seen was on a Jewess. All lace, buttons and strings. Made my hands shake."

"Why didn't you let her take them off herself?"

"Ba. That's not the style."

"Who says? ... lie down and smoke, and watch. She lets them go and they fall. Then she takes them on her right foot, on the toe-nails, without using her hands. She gives them one, and away they go!"

"That's taste. Down here in China, the girls wear cotton knickers right down to the knees, with laces round. Like kid's clothes; makes you feel sorry for them."

"Cotton ones are better than those nylon ones they sell everywhere now, even in the grocer's shops. Remember those things housewives used to wear thirty or more years ago?"

"No?"

"How to explain – big drawers. Wide, with an opening in the middle."

"How d'you remember? You were a child."

"From nine years old I could never leave women's dirty washing alone, wherever I found it."

"What are you saying, eh? First time I've heard of such a thing."

"That's the least of it ... there are other things."

"Me, I like to watch. That Ciné Cochon in Marseilles ... then there's the Teatro Bataclan in Buenos, with live shows. And a woman comes up to you as soon as she hears you breathing heavily. All moans and groans, from one end to the other."

"Hey, remember those houses with men, in Marseilles?"

"Ones who were that way inclined?"

"No, not at all. For women to go and get what they fancied. Know what happened to me once? I had this friend, Minas. A stoker; generous chap, but lazy. He got fed up with shovels and ash-rakes and went to work in one of those places. Had proper papers, from the Police. Well I went to the back door one day to see him. The boss, a

116

Spanish guy, liked me, because I'd given him some cigars. 'Come into the salon and see,' he said. 'If a customer comes, beat it.'

"Sitting on the sofas were a black guy from Morocco, a Mexican, and two Whites. All wearing blue shirts and white trousers. And suddenly, boys, a load of American women rush in. Before I could get away, one of them takes me by the hand. She had a silk scarf round her head. I tried to get away, but the Spaniard pushes me and I find myself in one of the rooms. She takes off her scarf. More than seventy years old, all worn out – and ugly. And expecting what she'd come for."

"What did you do?"

"Whatever she told me – she gave me a dollar when she left."

"Too much. Have you been to this place we're going before?"

"No. Further up, in Amoy."

"D'you think there'll be any brothels?"

"Don't know … forget it. They've closed them everywhere, except there's some left in Beirut. That's why the world's full of pox; have you seen the deck-apprentice?"

"Yes. Looks like he's got it. He's always whispering with the wireless officer. And *he's* like treading in shit. Hey, Polychronis, stop picking your nose, it turns me over. D'you think they'll ever put doctors on the cargo ships?"

"What are you talking about, Linatsa, are you crazy? What for, to eat and make manure?"

"Sometimes just to *see* a doctor can make you feel better."

"You don't know what you're talking about, I tell you," said the carpenter. "I was on the mail ships and I saw the doctors up close. You think a good doctor would go on a ship? Once a passenger got ill. Forty-five years old, strong as an ox. Three days later we threw him in to measure how deep the Indian Ocean was."

"Well, he was probably going to die anyway. Not the doctor's fault."

"He had pneumonia. Didn't even give him one of those new injections; couldn't be bothered. Another one spent the whole time lying in an armchair reading books about trees. Got annoyed if you asked him for an aspirin. You'd say 'Doctor, I've got a pain in the side' and he'd sigh and say 'Me, too.'

"One night in Genoa a worker fell in the main tank. They woke the doctor up. First thing he said was 'Oh, *now* he decided to fall in? How can I go down there? I'll fall too.' He was an old man, a wreck. We were shouting from above 'Hold on, the doctor's coming.' Three men lowered him down. Took another three to pull up the worker, dead.

"Another time some woman from First Class called him. 'Doctor,' she says, 'I've got ...' he didn't let her finish, he sighed and said 'Ah, me too.' 'But Doctor, I'm bleeding, you know? From down here.'"

Linatseros burst out laughing; "Come on, that's too much."

"And he had funny tastes, too, the old queer. We spied on him one night. Weird. Ever hear of something they call the 'Spring'?"

"Where they use pulleys?"

"No. See, you take ..."

Four quick double bells cut their talk, and all three of them ran out on deck.

As soon as the bell stopped two sweating men, covered in soot and oil, came out of Number One Hold. They wore dock-worker's trousers, sleeveless vests, and black slippers full of holes. One of them, Remouskos, sat down on the rim of the hold and wiped his forehead with his handkerchief. He'd be about fifty, but looked sixty. Lame, with a hollow face, and a thin body scorched by fire. The other, Tenedios, same age, well-built, chewed the corner of the tattered scarf he wore round his neck. His arms were covered in tattoos.

"What're you sitting down for?" said Tenedios. "Let's go and wash. Are we going to eat like this?"

Remouskos got up with some effort and they went towards the fo'c'sle. There was a light off-shore wind blowing. The greaser who was on watch with the deck-hand, a dirty old sod known as Kareklou, stood at the rail looking towards land.

"Good times tonight," murmured the deck-hand. 'soon be there; get your vaseline. I'll have two."

"Yes ... tighten it up," laughed the greaser, "and then we'll rub you with a match, and we'll have you bent double for three weeks, like that time in Lome. Get lost."

"Me, eh?" he said angrily, "Me? I bet you. I'll put down scores."

"Just take a few photographs of the ones you know, that'll be enough for you. The condition you're in you're only fit to be a madam. Remember Perivolaria?"

"Do I remember her? I had her for two years. And Papyro in Kerkyra, and Lemonia with the fat arse in Syria. Karavo, Doubina ... now *they* were madams. Not like the ones today."

"And Kareklou? She's the one you knew best. Kareklou from Othona."

"On your mother's ... You china piss-pot! There!" and he punched him.

The stoker, a skinny Syrian, called them: "Dinner time!"

Remouskos sat on the hatch, Tenedios next to him, and they started to eat from the same plate: rice and meat.

"You're not eating mate," said Tenedios after a while. "Only one for my three."

"Call this food? ... There'll be letters. You think the pilot'll bring them?"

"How should I know? ... Another torture. Always late, often so wet you can't read them. And still worse, you get a bunch of letters from the last trip, and the new ones are in some drawer in Port Said. Who thinks of you? What a mess. Last year I spent Easter at home. I was sitting and eating with the old lady. Knock on the door. Postman. A letter covered in rubber stamps and crossings-out, been following me: Savitzo, Rosario, Halifax, Motzi. Never caught up with me at any of them. 'Tear it up,' my wife says. 'No,' I said, 'leave it sealed. I'll take it with me and read it out at sea, on some feast day, when I haven't had one for ages.' We laughed."

"You think it's a joke?" muttered Remouskos. "It nearly drives me crazy. Haven't had one for five months."

"But you had a telegram, old thing, at sea ..."

"What use was it? 'I am in sound health.' Was it the truth?"

"You mean you could tell if it was the truth if it was in a letter?"

"Letters are something else. If something's going on – touch wood – and they don't write it, you can still tell. I know my daughter's letters from way off. Lovely writing. And the things she says! In the last one she said 'Daddy, don't tire yourself. Eat well, enjoy yourself,' and underneath 'In a few years I'll look after you. You'll lie back and you won't have to do anything.'"

"How old is she?"

"Just on thirteen. Reads books. Not rubbish, not magazines. Deep books. Last winter I was home for a month, and she read to me every evening. I tell you, the torment will send me off to the other world, Tenedios."

"Don't talk like that, you old misery. Why?"

"Because … because it's … how to put it? … I was away during the occupation. She was four when I left. How could a woman with a child manage? Beans and greens. If they could have had the tinned stuff I was throwing in the sea during the war! Hard times. She got hurt once, on some bamboo … the wound closed up long ago, but there it is, the mark of it … she doesn't walk so well on the left leg. 'It's fine,' she says, 'Doesn't bother me at all, father.'"

The stoker hauled up a coffee-pot on a long wire and put it down beside them.

"Have you finished?"

"Yes."

"I'll wash your plate up with mine, don't worry. Cheer up, we'll be there soon." He gathered up the things and left.

Tenedios stroked his big moustaches. "Whichever way you look at it it's bad, cold, and black. But there are worse things. I brought up a boy, there at home – that's to say, to tell the truth, his mother brought him up – when she was giving birth I was smoking a narghilé. That's the injustice of it. We ought to feel a few pangs ourselves, below the belt, when our women give birth. He was three years old when I next went back after a voyage. 'Tough kid,' my wife says; 'won't calm down.' I quarrelled with her. He had a catapult; used to take people's hats off. Once he got some coconuts, cut them in half, hollowed them out, tipped pitch in them and shoed three cats. You'd hear them at night on the paving-stones, clip-clop, clip-clop, like horses. I caught him, made him understand very clearly! Took him three days to clean up their paws.

"When he was eighteen he was the craftiest kid in the neighbourhood. Worked as a carpenter. He'd never pass a beggar and leave him hungry. When he was twenty, during the occupation, he thumped some German in Omonia square for pushing him. Smashed his face in, pulled his trousers off and shoved his pistol up his arse. Well you can guess what happened. Three of them emptied their guns into him. They told me that as he was dying he stuck his tongue out at them. Tough kid. I'd rather he was lame in both legs, blind, paralyzed. Just to have him still, to see him ... did you say something?"

The other sat with his head bent. The ship's cat was sitting on his knees, scratching itself.

"What're you doing, Diamantis?" asked the wireless officer.

The cadet spun round, surprised. "I'm trying to iron a shirt, but ..." He'd spread a blanket on the hatch of the coal-bunker, the damp shirt on top. He'd corked up a bottle of boiling water from the engine – an old sailor's trick – and was trying to use it as an iron.

The wireless officer stood and looked at him: there were red marks under the sweat on his forehead, and his blond hair was thinning. His face looked longer.

"I'm getting myself ready," the boy said; "Are we going?"

"Without fail. This time tomorrow, we'll be ..." he hesitated – "We'll know. Stop struggling with that bottle, I've got a silk shirt, never been worn. Doesn't suit me; let's go and get it for you."

"But ... well ..."

"It's a present. Come on, let's go."

"Just a moment ... if ... I mean, if I've got ... if I'm ill, will I have to stay ashore?"

"Are you crazy? It's not in your legs! We'll get injections; I'll do them for you."

"Are they very expensive? I've got some money, but I don't know if it'll be enough."

"Diamantis. If you got to be Captain or First Mate, and an apprentice or anyone else needed something urgently, what would you do?"

"But ..."

"No buts. Let's go."

"Hey! Up forward! Rope-ladder and a line on the windward side!" came the call from the bridge.

"In position!" shouted Captain Panayis from the fo'c'sle.

The Captain was wearing white linen, four gold stripes on each cuff and gold braid on the peak of his cap. Fifty years old, tall, plump. Cheeks the colour of dead roses, yellow circles round his cow-like eyes. A beer-gut poking out of his half-open shirt. "Dead slow," he called to the First Mate, who was holding the handle of the engine-room telegraph.

The engine-room answered; a musical ring.

"Stop engines," said the Captain after a little while.

The engine-room answered and the *Pytheas* lost way.

"Steady as she goes."

"On course," answered Linatseros.

The pilot cutter drew alongside.

"Diamantis, take down the 'G' and hoist the 'H'."

"Coffee and cognac for the pilot," ordered the Captain.

The Chinese pilot came up on to the bridge: "Tsigoua Ho. What engine? Draff?"

"Twenty-three."

"O.K. Dangerous cargo?"

The Captain bent and whispered something; the Chinaman smiled. "How many tugs want?"

"Two."

"Speed?"

"Eight."

"All right."

They paid out the hawsers to the tugs.

"Starboard," said the pilot.

"Starboard," repeated the Captain; "Ready on the port side for making fast."

The ship entered the basin. The breeze smelt of dung, rotten seaweed, and war.

To right and left, hundreds of moored sampans. A body dressed in khaki floated by on the current. Unless it got tangled in the river-weed it should reach the open sea. Far off could be heard the sound of artillery fire.

The wooden pilings came in sight, covered in graffiti, as in so many harbours: a diversion of sailors as they painted the ship's sides. Now they could be made out: ahead, written in Dutch, "Got here in a fifty-year-old floating coffin. Long live Holland!" Further on, in Greek: "Worthless port. Filthy wine. The women are thieves, they stink and they've got lice." Still further on, French: "10,000 miles from Place Pigalle. Sale." And somewhere else: "Carry a knife at night."

"We're nearly there; why aren't you smiling?" a passenger asked me one midday, as we reached harbour after a long journey.

I looked at her; I hadn't understood.

"Sorry, I should have explained. I mean, why aren't you happy we've arrived? Your eyes look just the same as when we set out."

"Maybe because this isn't my home port," I answered.

"That must be it. I should have guessed."

It seemed to me that, for all that I hadn't been sincere, I'd given her the right answer. Years later an Indian woman asked me the same question when we saw the lights of Piraeus, coming back from the South. Luckily that moment I was called away to do something ... Our home port. The worst in the world. You're back. On the jetty, the agent's looking for you. He tells you, half swallowing the words.

"You mean, I've got to get off?"

"Yes."

"Is the ship impounded?"

"No."

"So someone else is taking over?"

"Yes."

"You could have sent us a message out at sea, so I'd have my things ready. She's off again in three hours. Tell me, did I do something, that they're taking me off?"

"How should I know? Orders from the office. I do what they tell me, I'm just an employee."

Then you sit like a fool and look round you. You lived in this cabin six months, a year ... now you're a stranger. You open the drawers, fill your kit-bag first. Then your suitcase, then a small bag. You're finished. But there's a heap of little things left over. You stuff them in. Now something to leave behind in a corner – old sailors' tradition – I'll leave that iodine, this half-used course of bismuth. Who knows. Someone else might leave a sixpence, an odd pair of socks.

You come out onto the jetty. The sleeve of your uniform, with the stripes showing, is hanging out of your case. Wear it tomorrow, go for a stroll round Syntagma square. If it's carnival time, there'll be people going up and down. But is it worth it? Patched and stained. Oil, paint, salt, sweat. Blood. "Tell us a story about sailors." Well, listen, madam: the next day you go to the union, and you're last, behind two hundred, all waiting for a ship. Shit. You've got sixty-three drachmas left. You're nothing, off the ship, a mile from the sea. For months you sit on a park bench, wearing out your trousers. You cut down on your cigarettes. Cut out coffee altogether. All you've got left are your worry-beads. The string breaks and you lose half of them.

You're better off abroad when you haven't got work, people who know you can't see you and shake their heads. The Sailors' Rest in Cardiff – knife and fork fixed to the table with little chains. Soup served with something that looks like an enema. At night you sleep in your clothes, so you don't lose them. When the sun shines, you lie on the grass in Roath Park and stare at the ducks. Not a woman comes near you ... You hang around Bute Street, learn to play dice ... once someone started with a shilling and won five pounds. Didn't put it in his pocket, he was so proud he kept stopping to count it. On the corner some Cuban grabbed it off him – broad daylight – and ran off, and he was left staring at his empty hands. Then the day comes to leave, you get your papers, and then the fun starts: Sailors' House, Immigration, Insurance, Doctor, Port Authority – all in order? You get ready. Get your sub and pay what you owe. Half-dead by the time you get aboard. Weigh anchor, set off. And always you live with the fear they'll take you off the ship. It's a mania, you'll say. Maybe. There was a sailor once who waited two years to get a ship. Soon as he got his papers, he tore them up and went back to Terpsithea Park. When the sun went down he killed himself.

"Port anchor!"

The bosun let off the brake and the anchor dropped, making a lot of noise. A single bell measured the fathoms of chain: one, two, three …

"Hold the chain."

"Held."

"Wind back."

"Done."

"Tell the stern tug to pull more," then "Two hawsers ashore." A pair of thin lines were thrown over, drawing behind them the thick hawsers. Four or five Chinese ran and looped the eye-splices over the bollards.

"Make fast fore and aft. Set springs … slowly on the lines."

They drew gently against the wooden jetty. The First Mate stopped to talk to the bosun at the bottom of the bridge companionway: "Everything done? Lights?"

"Everything."

"Rat guards set?"

"Those too. Did they bring the letters?"

"Yes, the pilot's got them."

"Did you hand them out?"

"You're worrying me just like the others, Vangeli. I told him twice, 'People are waiting.' 'Let them wait,' he says. 'Give them to me,' I said, 'and I'll hand them out.' But no, no."

"Snakes and a singleside strike him. Know why he does it. The mule can kick him with all four hooves— does it to torture people."

"So he can take the stamps off."

"You're joking."

"I swear it on my own eyes; may I not live to walk on dry land. Didn't you know?"

"The doctor's here," someone shouted. They set off in a hurry; "Lower the gangplank." It came down, screeching, onto the quay.

A little later the First Mate came out of the saloon and shouted to the bosun "Don't take the quarantine flag down. Get the crew together in the stern for vaccinations."

"More problems. Smallpox?"

"No. Plague."

"Right. I'm on my way."

The First Mate stood scratching his head. The third officer came up, on his way from the stern. "Did you hand them out?"

"Later."

"Fine, doesn't bother me."

"So why did you ask? Want to make something of it?"

"Oh, just out of habit." The third officer went and leant on the rail, and the First Mate walked off, limping.

Two stokers, the cook's mate and a coalier stood outside the saloon. They beat loudly on the door. The Captain's steward, tall and thin, white haired, with a squint, opened the door a crack: "What is it, boys?"

"Our letters."

"Not now. He's talking with the pilot and the doctor."

The coalier reached out to him and pulled an envelope from his pocket: "So what's this, then? Tell him to give them to you right now, or we'll go in and get them ourselves."

The door closed.

"Little bastard!— needs swimming lessons."

The door opened again: "Tell the others to come here, not to the stern. For vaccination and letters."

"Any for me? Did you see?" asked the cook's mate.

"Don't know."

The crew went in, two by two, without any fuss. They came out with their sleeves rolled up, pressing pieces of cotton wool to their punctured arms. Some were holding letters. They scattered to find quiet corners. One read aloud, another moved only his lips, another smiled. Remouskos came out with his head hanging. The cook's mate came up to him: "No letters again?"

"She didn't answer."

"I got five. Two of them last year's. Want half of them?"

Remouskos went off to the stern, sat on a bollard and took out a cigarette. Tenedios nudged him gently; "May your dead be forgiven. Read it for me."

Remouskos took the letter and started to read it by the remaining fading daylight. Flocks of birds came to roost on the rails and hatches.

On shore two men from the agents, and a few customs officers, were waiting. They all wore long white shirts hanging outside their trousers down to their knees. Someone leant by a porthole, doing business with a black engine-hand. A customs offer chased him away, swearing.

A woman stopped at the gangplank. She was holding a flower; a Chinese sunflower. A dog stood on its hind legs to rest its forepaws on her.

Waking up for the first time in a strange country. You rub your tired red eyes, your sight's clouded. People you never imagined. You love them. You do business with them, get to know them. You leave. At home, for a while, you remember them, as you're going to sleep. Memories are only worth having when you know you'll be going on another voyage. The worst, most hopeless loss is to be stuck in your own country, living on memories.

In some Gothic churches, on the backs of the pews, you can find obscene carvings. Filthier than the ones on the stone temples in India. The anonymous wood-carver was working for his own amusement, fed up with working for others, for piety, for ideas. But no, not for amusement: to leave his own mark. There is nothing in the world that can't happen. The most impossible, the most fearful. It's enough that someone thinks of it.

The best coffee I ever drank was in Moka, the best tea in Colombo. When I asked the Indian waiter for a third cup, he got angry: "You want to lose what you've gained?" The worst coffee I ever took home for my mother, I bought in Moka, and the worst tea in Colombo. From the same shops where I'd drunk them.

The painter Petridis, a refugee from Russia who shined shoes in Drapetsona. He'd painted his shoe-shine box in the style he'd been taught in the Moscow Polytechnic. A little oil tempera picture, showing a few olives in a piece of wrapping-paper, two onions – one of them sprouting – a piece of black bread and a few olive-stones. But the theme of the picture was something else; a lamp with a broken glass. There was no room for it in the composition, it stayed outside, hanging on the wall, obliquely lighting the table.

A winter sunset in Martigues, the girl beside me talking incessantly. Nets hanging, fishermen's houses with dried sea-horses and starfish nailed on their doors. When we want to get to know a place, listen to music, visit a museum, we shouldn't have a woman with us. It's not worth sharing anything with them; not even your bed. They interrupt you, crudely, like soldiers, like sailors. "Let's have some oysters ... Oh, look! 'La Venise Provençale.' Let's eat at Crespi's."

Shame: she hadn't seen the shade that rose from the canal and walked beside us. It was he, who from childhood had felt the damp in his slim fingers, the fog in his nervous nostrils. The box with the colours hung at his waist, the easel under his arm. Since early morning he'd been painting the mist on the harbour waters, that he loved more than the shores of his own country, and now he was tired.

"Shut up. Listen and learn, brainless, adorable girl. Your hair fights with the left-over colours, the lead-grey struggles with the purple and swallows it. Now he kneels suddenly, opens the box and, on the fluffy back of a woollen vest, paints the rotten barges, the smell of fish, and your hair. He's sombre, just as he was in that miserable fenced-round house in Attica. The painter of Missolonghi and Provençe, Michael Oikonomou."

Sailors are acrobats. They wear seamen's overalls or faded khaki, covered in spots of red, green, black, white. They can go to the top of the mast on a rope, without their feet touching anything. They can hang for a moment by their teeth, in crossing a stretched rope, a current rushing beneath them. Their hands are worn, covered in cuts and scars. Some have a finger missing, eaten by a pulley-block, a steel cable, a winch. It lay on the deck, warm, a while. The cat sniffed it and ran off. The ship's dog recognized it, licked it. Then it was swept away, with the other rubbish.

At difficult and dangerous times, I've heard sailors say, rubbing their hands, "And now, split open again, Maria." The name changes in each one's mouth. Eleni, Theodora, Elpida; whatever the mother's name. Two people are suffering at that moment; the mother and her child. The mother more. She suffers beside him, however far away he is. It's a second birth, tied by a thread to death.

When the ship rides at anchor, outside the harbour or in a river, they sit on the hatches and plait cords, with three, five, nine threads. Or they cover a bottle in plaited cords and paint it. They love colours. The bosun mixes the paints, to find the right colours. As they paint the ship's sides they play, painting something for themselves. And however much they wash, they always smell of rancid fish-oil, rust, and caustic soda. A smell the whores, and the seamen's mothers, love.

When you see someone, far out of town, leaning against a wall, smoking, or playing with his worry-beads, it'll be a sailor who's retired, dropped anchor.

In Port Sudan there's a tribe of tall skinny blacks, with tufts of frizzy hair on their heads, and wooden forks hanging from their necks to scratch themselves with. They wear just a pair of shorts, and work unloading the ships.

I was lying in my cabin, two fans going, half-dead with the unbearable heat. One of them came and knocked on the door.

"Me – Idomeneos – from Iskender – give clothes."

I gave him an old vest. He hugged and kissed me. I waited for him to go.

"Need paper," he said.

"What for?"

"English think steal – beat."

I wrote him a receipt. He still didn't go; he wanted it rubber-stamped. A bit later another one came:

"Me Kalchas." He got a pair of shoes, and a receipt. Then came Agamemnon, Protesilaos, Philip.

That night in some back street I saw one of them and he recognized me:

"Me Kriton – come with."

They'd told me Greeks got no trouble in that place, down as far as Djibouti, so I followed him. We went into a hut. A girl greeted us: she had a white cloth round her waist that covered her as far as her knees, and she was combing her hair in a mirror. There was a lamp burning in front of an icon –

"My sister – pretty – Maria."

The girl turned and smiled at me; she had wonderful teeth. They gave me a drink that smelt of pepper and nutmeg. Kriton lit a fire and put a pot of water on to boil. I got up from the empty crate where I'd been sitting.

"If you don't like her," my friend gave me to understand, "We can go somewhere else." He seemed offended.

I sat down again and waited for him to clear off. The girl spread a cover on the ground, sat down and beckoned me to come close to her. Kriton threw some seeds into a censer and the hut filled with smoke. He knelt down with his back to us and started to sing to himself.

A long time passed. I got up to go and pee. The descendant of the Macedonian was sleeping where he knelt. The girl gave me more of the same drink; it blistered my mouth. At dawn the three of us sat together to drink sage tea. I wondered if I ought to pay. I gave her ten shillings. She got up, poked around in a box and brought me a half-crown change. I told her to keep it. She held it up and pressed it to her hair, exactly the way the sailors' mothers do in Kephallonia when their sons bring them their first sea-soaked money. Then she took my hand and pressed it to her breast, her mouth, her forehead. She was young, fifteen years old; her name was Amira.

Has it ever happened to you to arrive at the docks, and your ship's left on a ten thousand mile trip, it's getting dark, fog's gathering on the river, and you're three hours away from your consulate? Not a penny in your pocket, your bag empty. And it's the sailor's worst sin. For years they point at you, "Him who missed his ship down in –"

Christmas Eve – however drunk you are, you sober up at once. You sit on an iron bollard and think. The workers are off, and pass by, indifferent. You strain your ears, hoping to catch a phrase in your own tongue. You leave the docks and wander about the working-class area. You look at the lights behind the clouded windows, the little lace curtains. A door opens and the smells of the house, kitchen smells, hit you. Right now your mother will be taking the almond biscuits out of the oven, and thinking of you. She's been crying since morning, but she hides it. She had a bad dream – a ship under a tree. "When shall I wash his clothes again –" Stained, unwashed, sea-wet –

Somewhere a piano's playing. For the third time you look through your pockets. Isn't that a shilling, down at your feet? You bend down – no. It starts to rain. You find an old air-raid shelter from the First War and go in. It stinks, but it's warm. You trip over people, and they swear at you. You sleep sitting up. Get up at first light. Someone's rolling a cigarette; he looks at you and curses. You go out, banging your feet. You find a damp cigarette-end – fifty yards on there's a flag fluttering, blue and white.

Quarter past nine.

"Yerasimos, we're going."

Yerasimos finishes the calculation, puts down his pen and gets up. The wireless officer is wearing a crumpled suit and a green trilby. The cadet waits outside.

"Well," says Yerasimos, "You'll have heard. We're off at three in the morning. They wanted to chase us out earlier, but it's not high water until three. Two feet less and we wouldn't make it."

"But where are we going?"

"Formosa, where else? Can't you see they've abandoned this place? It'll fall without a fight."

"But can't you hear the artillery?"

"Long way off. Didn't you notice they've got all the lights on, like a party? Didn't you see the English warships outside the harbour?"

"No?"

"Four of them, ready to take the leaders, and their own people."

"'Where there's death, there's animals.'"

"More like 'Where there's shit, there's flies.'"

Diamantis started to cough.

"Look, don't fool about. Keep your ears pinned back for the whistle. Four long ones, and that's it. Just a moment, what's that on your head? Why don't you throw it away?"

The wireless officer pulled back; "Don't touch it! I wear it for luck."

"Antique. Why don't you get a cap?"

"I'll get a cap when I haven't got a ship. When I'm sick, or they've sacked me."

"What rubbish you talk. Hurry up then. The cars are all requisitioned. Take a couple of rickshaws, and don't hang about. Good luck."

Yerasimos turned out the light in his cabin, went down the companionway and took a walk from stem to stern. For all that he cursed it, he loved this iron ruin. He watched over it; he knew its faults and its good points. And he loved the crew, for all that he quarrelled with them. A good, honest man. "You shouldn't go against the sea," he'd say; "You have to respect it, live up to it."

He'd been torpedoed twice in the war. He was in love with his first cousin, but he'd never confessed it. They'd married her off to some good-for-nothing who beat her. Inside his pocket-watch he had a photograph of her taken when she was a child.

He leant on the wet rail and lit a cigarette; remembered how she used to play the mandolin. "Your coral lips ..." Evanthia ... He hit his leg, which had gone to sleep. He'd damaged it with an injection he'd done himself, out at sea: he'd hit a vein.

When he'd finished his cigarette he went up to his cabin, pulled the curtain across, and lay down on his back, in his clothes, the light still on. From somewhere on land a bird screeched. In the next cabin the Captain was walking up and down, talking to the chief mechanic. "You're always complaining," he was saying: "We've taken on coal four times this trip. You must have got at least forty pounds out of it."

"And you're so far behind?" said the mechanic: "Tips from the shipping-agent, from the water-suppliers."

"Oh, come on. We're carrying military supplies and you know it."

"What about ship's stores?"

"Are you saying I'm stealing supplies?"

"Ba— what are you saying— are we going to fight about food?"

"Fuck your faith!" the Captain shouted, hitting the table. "D'you want for anything? Is there anything you asked for and didn't get?"

"It's not me," the other muttered, "it's the crew."

"Who? Any complaints from anyone? Tell me what you want!"

"Oh, this kind of talk ..."

The Captain lowered his voice: "If you're talking about cheating ... in the Spanish war, a chap from Ithaca sold his cargo three times. To the reds, to Franco's lot ..."

"Fine! Well done! That's what I want to hear. Is there any chance?"

"Ba, no idea ... this is a different war."

The First Mate turned to the bulkhead that separated the two cabins and gave them the five fingers. Then he slept like a lamb.

"He's hiding, the crafty sod," muttered Linatseros, the deck watchman, as if talking to himself.

"Yes," answered the engine-room watchman, Antonis "The Headache", who was teasing the cat with a piece of rag on a string. "In our village we don't mind them, unless they come and make a noise outside the house. I don't believe in all that."

"Oh, yes? Well listen— you're new and you've got to learn. At dawn, when the fog had just cleared, Douroudous shouted 'Look, Captain Panayis, look!' 'What is it, stinker?' says the old man. 'Look, a turtle!' 'Shut up, boy, and don't look that way.' 'No, really, Captain – there it is!' The old man wouldn't turn to look, he just rubbed his hands together."

"You mean, the boy did something wrong?"

"Yes, idiot mailboat sailor. They're the worst creatures in the sea. No-one ever talks about them."

"So that's why ..."

"No wonder they call you headache. What more d'you want? Didn't they tell us to go as soon as we'd dropped anchor? You think that's good?"

"What's the connection?"

They were sitting near the gangplank. On the hatch was a plate with sardines and olives, nearby a coffee-pot. There was a sound of someone coming up the gangplank. Linatseros turned to look. "Luck's changing: we've got visitors. Did you shave?"

Antonis put down his piece of string and looked up. A woman came up and stood at the top of the gangplank. She stank of violets and garlic.

"What does she want?" asked Antonis-Headache.

"She's come to check us out. God, you're thick-headed. If you fancy her, take her, don't leave her standing there."

"Is it O.K.? I mean ..."

Linatseros beckoned her and she came forward, laughing, her eyes playing.

"Where can I take her?"

"Up to your bunk in the fo'c'sle. No, better go to the store-room. But don't set fire to the stuff. Don't smoke."

"But if I'm wanted?"

"Come on, you billy-goat. I'm here."

They set off for the store-room. "Congratulations!" he shouted after them. He sat down on a stool with his back to the land and started to sing to himself. The cat crept down the gangplank and disappeared among the pilings of the jetty.

Headache came back and bent to whisper "Have you got any ...?"

"Look in my locker; it's number four. They're in a Camel packet. D'you want me to come and show you how to ...?"

Suddenly a voice came from on shore: "Watch!"

"What's up?"

"Come down and take these cigars for the Captain." He'd come halfway up the gangplank; it was Polychronis.

"What's in that bit of paper?"

"Couple of cakes. One for you, one for Headache."

"Are they good?"

"Fresh. Smell of soya."

"Anything open out there?"

"Yes, a few places. And women! Cheap, too ..."

"Poor sod, you'll need help from the watchmen."

"Don't worry, I can manage. Go on, the Captain wants the cigars right away."

"O.K." He left, coming back a little later murmuring to himself: "I suppose that's what you smoke back in your village, you gypsy. Havana. Couldn't the pig have given me just one? ... he knows how to make people feel bad." He sat down on the hatch, but jumped up again at the sound of wild screaming. "What the devil's that?" Then he realized he must have sat on the cat, but now she was nowhere to be seen. "Ah! The whore, the hidden wound! She's disappeared." He called her name: nothing.

Headache arrived, out of breath. "Have you got two shillings?"

"Hang on ..." He searched his pockets. "Here you are. Going to have another go? Take these cakes, keep your strength up. Don't be long."

He had another look for the cat. "Hope that bloody Chinaman hasn't got hold of her."

He remembered Rokamvol and Ririka, and his face darkened. He'd rescued them from a ship and brought them up. In '36 they'd taken Yiannoulatos's *Haralambos* to the Tyne for a cargo of iron. In Rotterdam the Captain had said "Get rid of those animals, they'll bring us trouble." He hadn't listened; how could he just abandon them, there in the docks? He'd hidden them in a basket, with the idea of letting them out at night. They'd been found, and they'd made him bring them down to the engine-room: Linatseros first and the sanitary inspector behind. He'd strangled them with little ropes and then thrown them in the fire-box. With his own hands. He gets goose-flesh when he remembers ... He went and leant on the wet rail ... Headache's being a long time. In the bordellos when they get customers like that they bang on the doors of the rooms. The madams call them "Postage stamps."

The mailboat crews ... they disgust him. He'd spent time with them; actually he felt sorry for them. They went around with such long faces, from staying up all night. "I found her in quarantine," one of them said about his wife. "She had a pain in her kidneys and we didn't do anything," said another, and "They went and told her I'd got another woman in Volos and she kicked me out of bed," said a third, a stoker.

"If I had the best whore in the world," Barbar-Thodoros the bosun's mate told him once, "She'd cost me less than my wife."

"How come?"

"It's like this ... we get back Sunday and we're leaving again in the evening. I go home and we sit down and eat. The children don't move. Time passes ... I give the big one ten drachmas for the cinema and he's off. Fifteen to the next one, to fix his bicycle, and he goes too. Then another ten to the youngest boy for the football match, and he's gone. That leaves just the daughter. 'Go and visit your aunt.' 'Don't feel like it.' 'My girl, go and gather me a little camomile.' 'I've already done it, father, and I've dried it too.' Well she's crazy for sweet things. 'All right, girl, go and buy yourself a nice cake. Not from round here; take the bus and go to that place near the National Theatre.' Work it out, Linatseros: that's a hundred drachmas gone."

Headache came back, coughing. Beside him the Chinese girl. "You want her?" he asked.

"No, mate, let her go."

She waved them goodbye. As she went down the gangplank she tripped over the cat on its way back. She bent down, picked it up and kissed it. It began to purr like a boiling kettle.

"Bye, and if you're feeling dry in a year's time, write to me," called Linatseros, then "Come here, puss." He picked it up. "In the end, you just do what you feel like, don't you? Scratcher, arse-fucker."

"Was she Chinese?" asked Headache.

"How should I know? Women don't have any race from the waist down."

"How's that?"

"Oh, you're killing me."

"What a woman! First time ..."

"You're not going to tell me she was a virgin?"

"Listen ... By God! ... Know what she told me?"

"In what language, idiot? If it wasn't Greek, you couldn't have talked. Go and make a couple of coffees, and stop talking rubbish. And keep your mouth shut tomorrow or you'll be in trouble."

From the land came the sound of distant singing, with guitar and mandolin.

> 'We saw Cassandra sprawling in the streets."
> To Thanasis Karavias.

Splice steel cables with your teeth. Climb the mast and turn three times with its rotten white tip in your navel, like the sailors who've been years dead.

Starlight. The road cut through the middle of a rice paddy. Here and there lights shone from huts built on pilings driven into the mud. An unspeakable stench of rotting flesh wafted and faded, then returned a little further on, stronger than ever, unbearable. Not human, not animal. Near the houses, a stink of piss and shit. Crows roosted on rocks. A stray dog stood in the middle of the road, uncertain which way to go. All that could be heard was the heavy breathing of the two coolies pulling the rickshaws. In one of them sat the sailor with the green hat over his eyes. From time to time he lifted it, to see the white shirt of the other shining where he sat in the rickshaw in front. Suddenly all the stars fell so low that they hid one rickshaw from the other. They were fireflies.

The cadet had a fever; his temples were throbbing. He had his hand in his trouser pocket, feeling around. If he could, he'd have lit a match to look. It had started to get smaller yesterday, and to hurt. Now it would be the size of a firefly, the smallest of all. Or like a precious stone he'd seen long ago in Kasado Shima. He hadn't had enough money to buy it. He'd remember all this one day and laugh. It was all *his* fault, that know-all behind, him and the First Mate who was afraid of his own shadow. He thought of telling the coolie to stop and go back. Go and find the others. There was a house over there on the right, at the end of the paddy.

Suddenly the two rickshaws stopped. One of the coolies put his fingers in his mouth and whistled. A woman came out and put down two buckets of water. The coolies knelt down and drank, silently.

"Diamantis, where are you going back there?"

"Just a moment. I want a piss."

"Come and piss here. Come on, we're going."

"I'm thirsty," whined the cadet, "Can we ask for a little water?"

"Wouldn't do," he answered gently. "Come on, cheer up."

The coolies got back in the yokes and they set off again, in the same order. They were running more quickly now; the road had widened and there were tall columns at intervals on the right-hand side. Diamantis started to count them.

The rickshaws slowed down and drew alongside each other. The two coolies talked together, twittering like two doves making love.

"The boy wanted water."

"I heard, offspring of Han."

"Shall we tip them out?"

"Not a good idea."

"Are you afraid? They wouldn't be the first! None of their people saw where we were taking them."

"They're not carrying any money."

"Not for the money. Just because they're white."

"If they were land people I wouldn't say no."

"What's the difference?"

"Well ... they're like us. They pull iron across the sea."

"With their hands?"

"Worse. With their souls."

The wooden bridge creaked under their feet. The whites were fast asleep, dreaming. The younger coolie stopped.

"Come on," said the elder.

"You're afraid."

"Maybe. When I was your age, I'd killed three white consuls in Peking."

"You've been to Peking?"

"I was there four years, working in a brothel."

"Have you slept with a white woman?"

"Many times."

"What are they like?"

"Disgusting. An old woman of our race, with ten children, is three times tighter than a twenty-year-old white."

"How come?"

"It's the water. Didn't you know?— If they drank from our rivers—"

They'd crossed the bridge. The younger one stopped again.

"What's up? Tripped on a stone?"

"No. Let's turn back."

"Listen, that young sailor's sick ... did you go to school?"

"No, never."

"Well I'm telling you, you don't kill sick people."

"*They* do."

"I'm talking about us. Woe to us if we were like them."

138

"All right then. Let's go on."

Diamantis was dreaming. All the dragons he'd seen earlier in the town were chasing him, catching him up, licking him with their fiery tongues. There's a woman with them, in charge of them. Her hair is thin snakes, her eyes full of vipers, her body, from the waist down, animal fat, clay, and mud. Her hands ... like his mother's hands; the narrow ring with the green stone she'd leave on the marble in the kitchen when she went to wash the dishes.

The other sleeps ... with the palm trees of Sidon ... one afternoon, in Esnoun, where they sell women ... a girl, stolen in Lesbos, hides her nakedness with her hands. An old headman from Bousir examines her, starting at her feet, then higher, then the breasts. His gaze lingers. She lowers her head and weeps. The old man counts his money. The sailor throws a bag of gold at her feet and covers her with his tunic. The two of them board a ship for Greece.

A knife, swords, stilettos ... more than hands can hold ... is there no place left on his body for the last flashing blade?

He wakes, and rubs his hand. An old scar, that he loves. He'd been wandering about the docks one night in Rotterdam. A girl is leaning against the stanchions of a crane, eating rotten bananas. At her feet a crate, from the white ship that's unloading further down. The next crane's working; its spotlight shines on her, leaves her in the dark, shines on her again. She's ugly. Her dress is spattered with mud.

A sailor, wearing no shirt, draws near: "What's your name?"

"Dédée."

"Come and eat on the ship."

"Don't want to."

"Wait then; I'll bring you something."

"No. I know why you're being 'kind'. So you can throw me onto the bed afterwards. 'Turn that way.' 'Move over there.' 'Now like this.' ... I know you. When you've finished you light a cigarette and don't look back. It was a sailor who dragged me down ... for a handful of beads. He liked to see me cry. He got me drunk. When I was lying on my back with my legs up he took a lit cigarette and put it behind me, down there. Called his mate, and they played 'Odds and evens', pulling out the hairs on my ... Get lost! I spit on you! Filthy dogs!"

He made as if to stroke her hair, to console her. She grabbed his hand and bit it, like a mad dog. It hurt, but he didn't pull away. He loves that scar. Sometimes it itches, and he remembers her. The most honest woman he'd ever met ... he fell asleep again.

And the two of them dreamt that they'd tripped as they were going downstairs: the two rickshaws stopped at the same moment. The cadet was the first to jump out. To the left of the road, in a fenced-off field, was a grey two-storeyed house with lit windows.

The coolies lay down on their backs. "I'll count the stars," said the younger. "Me the fireflies," the elder.

The nurse took them into the hall and left. They stood waiting for some time. There was a vase of honeysuckle on a low table in the middle of the room. On the walls Chinese ink drawings, a coloured lithograph of Cézanne's "The Blue Plate", and a picture of the Charioteer of Delphi.

The girl came back; "Please sit down. The doctor says forgive him, but he'll be a few minutes." She was un-made-up, as beautiful as a china doll; a joy to look at.

They stood in front of a bookcase. "Did you see her, Diamantis? What a smile! What would you do if *she* fell at your feet?"

Diamantis tried to smile. The door opened behind them and Doctor Ma Tuan came in, bowing. "Greek?"

"Yes."

"I am at your disposal." He spoke in English, with a slightly nasal pronunciation. He bent and adjusted the flower vase.

The wireless officer – an African would not have been jealous of his English – explained matters quickly, as best he could.

The doctor nodded, put his hand on Diamantis's shoulder and led him into the surgery – "And you may wait. I shall not be long."

"Look, Doctor, I believe that ..."

"Never mind the jokes," said the Chinaman, closing the door.

"Difficult customer," murmured the wireless officer. He turned to the bookcase and pulled out a book. He leafed through it, made a face, closed the book quickly and put it back in its place. "Devil take it—

whenever I look in a medical book I find my own symptoms." He pulled out another and started to read:

> Lo mio maestro disse: Quegli è Caco, che sotto il sasso di monte Aventino di sangue fece volte laco ...

"Hit it again." He turned to another part of the book.

> Lo copro mio gelato in su la foce trovo ...

The Chinese girl approached him apologetically: "One moment. The young man, your friend, wants you."

He followed her into the surgery. He saw Diamantis sitting on a low stool, his head hanging, holding his knees. There was a glass of lemonade beside him. "What's up, Diamantis?" and he tilted the boy's head up.

"He'll get over it," said the doctor. "We scraped a bit with the scalpel and it hurt. You sailors are cowards when it comes to illness. Here, drink." He gave Diamantis the glass, then went over to the sterilizer. He had his back to them; the nurse went out. The wireless officer opened a bottle that stood on a glass table next to him. There was a death's head on the label. He tipped some on his index finger and brought it up to each nostril in turn. Then he put the bottle back in its place and his hands in his pockets. He took a death breath ... Diamantis had recovered his composure.

The doctor approached them: "You'll have to wait at least two hours; please go to the sitting-room. Would you like coffee? Tea?"

"Coffee, if possible."

"I'll come and join you in a moment."

"But ... when d'you sleep?"

He smiled. "In the afternoons, for three hours." He was about thirty-five years old, taller than average, with fine, slim hands. He looked at his wrist-watch. "Just eleven," he murmured.

The cadet picked up a *Geographic Magazine* and leafed through it. The other put his finger to his nose again, half-closed his eyes and watched Diamantis, who was turning over the pages without reading them. "What the devil am I doing in this place, at this hour?" he thought to himself. "No-one took *me* anywhere when *I* caught it; I had to go through it alone. This time of night, I could be feeling up some Chinese girl, instead of ..." He regretted the thought at once. "The older I get, the more of a misery ... that's bad." He remembered another cadet – then, he'd have been the same age as this one. The linseed had caught fire in the Red Sea, and they'd opened the hold. He'd slipped and fallen right in. When they'd unloaded a month later, in Motzi, they'd pulled a mummy out of the hold. He'd plucked up the courage to go and take a look. Only the blond hair was unchanged. He'd loved the boy, just like this one, just like all those making their first voyage. Or like the girls whose mothers had left them in his charge on the *Corinthia*, and he'd kept them close by him all the way. Felt their foreheads to check for fever, held them when they were sea-sick, taken them to St Charles station for the train to Paris, and when they'd missed the train slept in the room next to them in the hotel, so they wouldn't be afraid. It had never occurred to him to try anything on with any of them. One of them had got him to take her to the streets with the "Bad women". He'd taken her to a café in the narrow streets behind the opera house. The women – they didn't have much work – surrounded her. One of them went to get her some sweets. They'd all complimented her on her French. They'd touched her, wanting to stroke her, they'd hugged her in the street, they'd kissed her hair. She'd squeezed his hand as they'd walked away towards the Cannebière, and he'd heard her sniff. "Have you caught a cold?" "No. But they're not so 'bad'," she'd answered, weeping.

Not one of those girls had ever sent him so much as a postcard.

He picks up a copy of *Life* ... "Can-can in Paris." He throws it down ... "Who was it told me ... what sod, what stool-pigeon ... said that Blanche's daughter had thrown off her nun's habit and was dancing the can-can in Montevideo ... but why should I care, in the end? The Mytilene girl died in childbirth last year in Athens ... whatever I touch turns rotten ... it doesn't die; it rots ..." He opens a *Paris Post* and reads. "Parfums de Coty" ... the girl in Antwerp. Her pillows and sheets smelt of "Styx". And then ... no ... I remember it well, but I don't want to ... when I was taking the dahlias and chocolates to her, in the hotel, to her whom I didn't know, though we slept in the same bed ... the woman who stopped me on the way, the fat, ugly woman, with painted lips, painted cheeks, painted forehead even ... she wore "Styx". No ... couldn't be ...

The doctor came in, smiling. He stoop up, Diamantis too.

"It'll be a while yet, sit down."

"Have you ever travelled?" the wireless officer asked, just for something to say.

"Yes. I was in Berlin for two years, then I went to England, and America for a while."

"Were you studying there?"

"Had to; no other way," he said bitterly, "But my grandfather, who was a traditional doctor, could cure things I can't, nor the Europeans with their new drugs."

"How's that?"

His face darkened. He said, through clenched teeth, "The first sick person in the world was Chinese. And naturally, the first doctor."

"But the Greeks?"

"The Egyptians ... the Greeks ... the bible's thousands of years later. You may know geography well, but you need history too. You said earlier you were Greek. I accept that."

"Is that supposed to be a compliment?"

He smiled; "I believe you entirely. But tell me, why aren't the whites who're incised on old gold coins, carved in marble on urns, why aren't they like the ones who live in Europe now? You don't remind me at all of the Macedonian. But if you look at the oldest Chinese coin, you'll see my face on it."

The other was in no state to get angry. He asked, avoiding the doctor's eye, "But cancer ..."

"Don't be in such a hurry. Last century the spirochaete killed twice as many people as cancer does today. And in a more horrible way. That's forgotten now. The two of you crossed the sea, terrified, for no good reason. It's ten days' work."

"It can be cured for certain?"

"Yes. The new ... are you brave? Then come with me." He opened a door and went into the darkness. A little light spilt in from the hall. In the middle of the room could be made out an operating table covered with a sheet. The Chinaman touched a switch and the table was flooded with light. With a pair of forceps he pulled the sheet down from the top. A mass of mincemeat where the face should be. No nose, no eyes, no lips. A pulp; a gaping open wound. To right and left, curls of chestnut hair.

Suddenly they heard a faint moan, as of a distant ship's siren in the fog. The doctor turned round quickly: "Go back and wait," he said to the cadet severely, "I didn't invite *you* in here." He shut the door.

"Lupus," the wireless officer murmured.

"Don't talk nonsense. Lupus can be cured. This is an illness as old as China. It destroys only the face. Look:" He pulled the sheet right down. A fine, slim, clean body. "Not a mark," continued the Chinaman; "Look as closely as you like."

"Cover her up," said the other "She'll get cold."

"She stopped feeling cold, or shame, an hour before you came."

"Is she Chinese?"

"But can't you see? You can tell straight away, just from the pelvis. She was French, from the North. She'd been to all the American hospitals, tried all the new drugs, with no improvement. They brought her to me yesterday."

"Is that what killed her, then?"

He didn't answer, just looked at him seriously. The other lowered his eyes as if ashamed.

"If you're still here tomorrow afternoon, come, and I'll tell you the name of the illness, and its cure."

"How's that?"

"There's an old man down by the river who knows. He'll be coming at dawn; he's a friend of mine. The microscope shows nothing. D'you understand?"

A bomb fell somewhere nearby and the house shook. The doctor pointed north: "They're on their way. Neither they, nor the others who're leaving, love humanity. In the end, it's the starving who're in the right."

"Why don't you leave?"

"Forgive me, but that's my business. Let's go." He turned out the bright light. The wireless officer blinked and stood motionless; the doctor took him by the shoulders and led him into the hall. Diamantis wasn't there. They stood in front of the Cézanne.

"D'you like it?" asked the doctor.

"Yes … we've progressed since then."

"*They've* progressed. Picasso, Kandinsky, Klee. Giants! Just as well they didn't *talk* about painting."

"What d'you mean?"

"From Giotto to Dalí, the greatest painters have been the worst teachers. The truth came from the dealers surrounding them."

"You're right."

"A mediocre painter can tell us in words how he works. A great creator, never."

"Why?"

"Because he's drunk. He can take a piece of paper in his hands, an empty cigarette packet, a handkerchief, and play with it a while, conversationally, as it were – ill-treat it, in his own way – and abandon it. And if the person who finds it has vision, he'll feel its breath, rejoice in its form. If not, he'll throw it in the rubbish. D'you understand me?"

"Almost."

"Sorry. I have work to do." He went into the surgery.

"Where's the boy got to?" the wireless officer wondered. He wanted to scratch himself, just under the eye, but resisted the urge, remembering … He heard footsteps on the stairs. The cadet came in, smiling, his face shining: "I went with the … she showed me a collection of butterflies, d'you want to see them?"

"No."

"Will we have to wait much longer?"

The doctor came out with the nurse and they went down the stairs. As their footsteps receded, the wireless officer got up and opened the door of the surgery.

"Where are you going?"

"To take a look … listen, take it easy."

He came back a moment later, his nostrils twitching.

"Did you see? Have I got …?"

"Sleep, if you can. I'm sleepy myself. I didn't manage to find out."

The cadet looked at him strangely. He took off his white shirt carefully and hung it on the back of a chair. It was crumpled, soaked from the humidity. He sat on another chair, his arms folded. His chin fell to his chest; he was asleep.

To Tatiana Milliex.

Catherine ... the redhead from Glasgow. We were anchored off Melbourne; she came aboard at midnight.

The cyclone, coming up from Tasmania, had broken our hawsers twice and come close to smashing us against the wooden pilings of Williamstown.

She was wearing a red raincoat with a hood. Handed in her papers and hurried down the stairs to first class. I noticed her: a little bright red face, nose the size of a thimble. I heard her swearing at the porters. The door of her cabin shut with such a bang it frightened the whole watch.

We set sail at dawn; the pilot never came to take us out. We had eighty passengers, but didn't see any of them until we were off Cape Leeuwin; for five days and nights we might as well have been on a cargo ship. The stewards served them in their cabins.

"Someone put the eye on us in port," the bosun muttered; "Only way to get calm weather is to throw all the queers overboard."

"Better start with you, then," one of the cabin-boys shouted.

The deck was deserted. Only the Scots woman, in a big coat and rubber boots, went up and down from stem to stern, smoking like a coolie, knocking back four or five Drambuies a day and sticking her tongue out at the sea.

"It's that bad-tempered woman who's troubling the sea," Androyannis said to me one morning. "She's crazy I tell you. 'Bring me some kippers,' she orders me yesterday morning in her cabin. I bring them and she sniffs at them. 'Take them away and cook them some more.' I come back. 'Bring me my shoes— no, not those.' Well there were seven pairs under her bed; I felt like hitting her over the head with them. Know what the whore does every day? Leaves the hot water tap running and goes out. I told her about it yesterday; 'That's

146

how I like it,' she says. And when she presses the bell you'd think she'd nailed it down. Why doesn't she just fire a pistol when she wants the steward, like a rich Scots princess? It's shameful, but I'll tell you anyway, you're from the same place as me: yesterday morning, when she'd gone to the bathroom, I went in to tidy her cabin. Full of smoke, cigarette-ends on the floor, and two holes big enough to get your head through burnt in the blanket. Her knickers just tossed onto the pillow. How to describe them – like old oil-skins they were so dirty. I picked them up with a stick. I go to plump up the pillow, it's soaking wet. If three people had been crying on it it wouldn't have been that wet. I felt sorry for her. Just a kid; seventeen ... what the devil's wrong with her?"

... And where's Androyannis now? He loved me more than I can say. Crafty sod; he'd sell you a piece of seaweed for a silk tie and you'd thank him for it. And secrets in your ear ... "The couple in number four had a good time last night; they've broken the bed ... the French woman in eighteen's got her period ... That Pole's a topographer, you should see his sheets! Like maps! Well, he sleeps naked, the mule ... the old Australian woman with the glasses hasn't been for a shit for seven days; she'll explode ... that Belgian pisses in the wash-basin." Then he'd reach into his pocket; "Here, take a pear, mate, to eat while you're on watch."

It was morning when we arrived at Fremantle. I got dressed and went to go down the ladder. I had my left arm in a sling. Before I'd got down the first rung, someone tapped me on the shoulder. I turned back. The Scots woman was standing there, looking at me with her deep blue eyes. She was holding a heap of letters and ten shillings: "Excuse me, can you post these for me?"

"Give them to the agent," I told her.

"He's gone; I missed him."

I turned away; she called me back: "You'd be doing me a favour."

I took the letters and started to go down. Half-way down I heard her calling "And collect my letters."

"Up your mother's, you stinker," I muttered without turning round, and jumped onto the jetty. An hour later I saw her in a Chinese place, right opposite the Post Office, drinking milk.

In the evening we set sail for Colombo, and after four days we were off the Cocos Islands. Calm weather. We'd come from polar cold to tropical heat. We left our cabin doors wide open, to get a bit of air.

As soon as my watch was over I went to lie down; my legs were shaking. I stopped at the door: there was the Scots woman, at my little table. She'd spread out more than a hundred reproductions, mixing up the fresco-painters with the Cubists, Renaissance with Impressionists, Lautrec with Rafaelo. The blood rushed to my head; I felt like cursing her.

She got up and gave me her hand. "I was waiting for you," she said, with an angelic smile: "I want to thank you. Sit down."

I obeyed, like the best boy in the class. I'm sure I smiled too.

"I was looking through your books. D'you mind?"

"Not at all, help yourself ... will you drink something?"

"Whisky and milk."

The steward brought the drink on a tray.

"Aren't you drinking?" she asked.

"No."

"Why not?"

"I drank plenty before."

"Pity; we won't make good company."

"Where are you leaving the ship?"

"In Genova, if I don't change my mind ... I finished school this year and I'm making my first trip. I went to the Dutch East Indies and Australia. Now I want to go to Brazil, and further down. My father's arranged letters of credit for a year." She was smoking one cigarette after another; she kept changing the subject and forgetting what she'd said. She fiddled with whatever her fingers lit on; she must have lit the lighter fifty times: a Ronson I was taking as a present for a friend in Greece.

"When will we reach Colombo?" she asked me.

"Tomorrow evening."

"Will you be going ashore?"

"Definitely."

"D'you know the city?"

"I've been there eighteen times."

"Shall we go together?"

"Delighted."

"What time of night's your watch?"

"Twelve to four."

She got up and shook hands. She was wearing shorts; she had skinny legs with fine red down on them.

"Night ... I wish I'd been a boy."

"So you could be a sailor?"

"No. You sailors disgust me."

I thought about her once or twice during my watch that night. I liked her a lot. If she fancied me, she'd tell me by the time we reached Colombo. But why would she want me? There was a crowd of fine young men around her.

When my watch was over I went and had a bath. I went into my cabin naked and reached for the light-switch. A hand grabbed mine: "Don't be afraid, it's me, Catherine. I want to talk to you."

I saw her in the moonlight, stretched out on my bunk. I sat on the edge, and she took my hand in hers.

"I'm listening," I said.

"You must help me."

"If I can."

"Can or can't, you *must*." Her voice, pleading before, became angry. She took my hand and put it on her belly. "Can you hear?"

"I can hear the sea against the ship's sides."

"Idiot. You don't understand. The child ..."

I pulled my hand away. "What d'you want of me?"

"I told you before. To help me."

"Explain."

"I've got to get rid of it."

"You've knocked on the wrong door. The doctor ..."

She sat up and covered my mouth with her hand. "I'm sorry I told you. I chose the wrong person; tomorrow the whole ship'll know about it."

I gave her the thermos flask to drink from. "What d'you want us to do?"

"I was hoping you'd tell me."

"Foot baths and quinine."

"Waste of time. I've taken Progynon. Won't come unstuck."

"I know what. You can stay in Greece, in an island. Your husband's away at the war ... when you have the baby, you leave it with some people I'll tell you about. You can send them money to look after it."

"Fool," she muttered; "I went with a black man."

"In that case, we'll go to Aden. I've got good friends there among my own people. We'll find a doctor. There are some French ones; everything'll be all right."

"In Aden! You're crazy. We've got to finish this thing in Colombo."

"I don't know anyone there who could help us. It's just whores, and black guys selling precious stones."

"Just the two of us. We don't need a third, it's dangerous— we'll go by ourselves. We'll look in a directory and find a doctor. Europeans are out of the question."

"Why?"

"My father's brother is someone important in Ceylon. Imagine if he finds out."

"Doctors never talk."

"You never know. Or would you rather we went to my uncle and asked *him* to help me?"

"Fine. Just as you like."

She lowered her head, and stroked my hair.

"Give me your word," she said, a little later.

"You have it."

"Are you afraid?"

"No. A year today, if I remember, I might be afraid, but tonight, tomorrow, the day after, I'm not. Off you go now; it's getting light."

She got up. "D'you want me to kiss you?"

"No. Day after tomorrow, when it's all over."

"I mean, as payment?"

"Shut up. You're crazy."

She spoke again as she left: "So we're agreed? Say yes."

"Yes. Go to the devil, yes."

I listened to her footsteps clattering across the deck. "I'll smash your face in ... but later, when it's done."

That afternoon the monsoon was shaking the palm trees on the shores of Colombo. We dropped anchor at dusk. Eight was striking by the time we could get away. The loudspeakers called

> Sailing on Tuesday morning promptly. Do not go outside the
> European quarter.

Catherine was first down the ladder. She was wearing trousers and a white silk blouse. I was wearing my old green trilby and a waterproof jacket.

"Take your raincoat," I told her; "It's going to rain."

"Stop playing the guardian."

The launch dropped us at the customs-house quay. We were greeted by the beautiful Tamil girl who sold tea to the tourists, and as soon as we got outside we were surrounded by barefoot pedlars: "Change money ... wanta gems ... gold ..."

The café of the *Grand Oriental* was empty, only the waiters, barefoot but with gold jewellery. We found a city directory and looked through it.

"That's it!" she said, pointing: "Third line down. We've found it. Write it on a bit of paper and let's go."

I beckoned a waiter, but Catherine pulled my sleeve: "Don't ask! let's go."

We got in a taxi. I told the driver only the name of the street, and he scratched his head. "If you can't remember," I told him, "I can sit in front with you and show you; I've been there often." The Indian made a sign to show he'd remembered.

We entered the Indian quarter. We passed a square, a new Buddhist temple, a big vegetable market. Then we were out in the country.

"He'll do fine," I said loudly.

"Yes ... he's been expecting us since this morning. Is he Indian?"

"His mother. His father's English, from Government House."

I called to the driver: "No further. This is Ivor Garden."

"Shall I wait?" he asked.

"No. We'll be staying here tonight, with a friend. Here."

"Chankiou."

We took an arbitrary direction, following the fence round the park. The driver shone his headlights on us.

"Go away, you cuckold ... mule ..."

The lights went out and the sound of the engine receded. Catherine took my arm; her hand was trembling a little. "I can't see a light," she said.

"Don't be in such a hurry. We'll see, as soon as we've got past the park."

We reached a little group of houses with a few scattered lights.

"There it is," I said: "The first one."

A two storey house, no lights. I lit my lighter to look for a sign, a bell. I pulled on a wire, and from inside came a chaotic sound, like lots of gongs playing together. The door opened. A weak light shone on the staircase. We went up, and another door opened. We went into a well-lit room. Hanging on the walls were an alligator, a cobra, and a bird. On the large heavy desk was a copper vase with a big yellow flower; it gave off an unbearably heavy scent. There were also a fat book, open, and a horoscope. Nearby, scattered along a shelf, were various instruments like those used by the doctors on whaling ships in the eighteen-fifties.

There was a man sitting with his elbows on the desk, looking at a glass ball, mounted on a wooden base, that was changing colour. He didn't so much as lift his eyes to us.

"Come on, let's go," I whispered in her ear. "This isn't who we're looking for."

Catherine held me back. We stood there waiting for about five minutes. Suddenly the man lifted his head and looked at us.

"I've been waiting for you," he said, as if reprimanding us: "You're late."

He was fat, dark-skinned, with big barbaric hands. He wore a yellow robe, like that of a Buddhist holy man, open to the waist. Below that he was hidden by the desk. On his hairless chest a sea-stone hung on a greasy cord.

"Go behind that screen and undress," he said to the girl.

I offered him a cigarette; he took it and put it in a drawer.

"Ready," the girl called.

The doctor went over. He was short, with fat bare legs and no shoes.

"Nick," called the girl, "You come too; I'm afraid. Come over here."

"You're in your fourth month," the doctor told her.

"Two and a half!" she answered angrily.

"Four," the Indian said again, softly.

"Doesn't make any difference," I muttered.

"Makes a big difference. The baby's head's nearly as big as mine."

We all went back to the desk. The doctor stood behind it and rested his hands, fingers spread, on the desk-top. He gazed at the glass ball.

"Well," said the Scots girl, "Can you do it?"

"Sure. I can do it in a quarter of an hour. You'll stay here tonight, and by tomorrow afternoon you'll be fine."

"Impossible. We have to leave as soon as you're done."

"That's dangerous. I'll send you in my own rickshaw."

"And your fee?" she asked politely.

"Twenty-five golden."

Catherine turned and gave me a shocked look.

The Indian went to the door, locked it, put the key in the pocket of his robe and went back to his place behind the desk.

"We haven't got that much," I dared to say. "If you can do it for twenty-five in paper money, go ahead. Otherwise we'll have to go. D'you understand?"

"Don't worry," he said, "I'll send someone with you to the ship. By the time you come back with the money, I'll have finished."

"What ship?"

"The one you came in, and that's leaving at dawn. You've got time."

Difficult situation, I thought. "It's not possible, doctor. Goodnight. Catherine, let's go."

The Indian was motionless except for his eyes. "You know the law of the land?" he said.

"Yes." I said. "And you do too, I think."

"There's a difference. You asked me. I refuse, and I denounce you. I'm in the stronger position." He bent to gaze at the ball.

"Open the door, doctor," I said. "You must be joking."

"Not at all. You'll give me the gold, and when I've finished you can go."

"But why! ... Have you got any money?" I asked the girl, who looked lost.

"Twenty-five in paper money and some small change. You?"

"Ten in paper."

"Thirty-five green ones," I told him.

"Twenty-five golden," he said, measuring his words.

"Let me think a moment."

The bastard smiled, pleased with himself. I put my hand in my pocket; I hadn't worn that jacket since I'd been in Naples. Our friend opened a desk drawer and looked inside. He put his hand in and released the safety catch. Then suddenly the desk spun round and he was down on his stomach, his right foot caught under the desk and a pistol lying within inches of his hand.

"Grab it," I told her, "Quickly!" Catherine picked it up.

Our man groaned like a wounded beast. A Neapolitan stiletto flashed in front of him: "Now give me the key, pig."

"I can't. Get my leg free."

The stiletto grazed his nose; I was on my knees: "The key."

"Take it," he said, throwing it from him and struggling to free his leg.

The girl still held the pistol as she gaped stupidly.

"Can you find some scissors?"

"Yes."

"Cut the telephone cord, quickly. As soon as I've opened the door, cut that wire on the wall. Wrap the scissors in your scarf first."

She did as I said. I opened the door, she cut the other wire, we went out, and I locked the door, putting the key in my pocket.

"Light a match," she said.

"Not a good idea. The stairs are just here."

We went downstairs and outside.

"Just a moment while I get my breath," she said.

"Not now. Follow me."

A coolie in white shorts appeared at the corner of the park, coming towards us. He ran past, and I saw him go in where we'd just come out.

"And now let's go. Doesn't matter which way."

The wind had dropped; there was a little thunder and lightning. We ran; she started to pant.

"Give me your hand."

"I can't, I've got the pistol."

"What, child? Throw it away, quickly!"

She threw it into a ditch.

We carried on running. There was no-one about. We reached the market. "We've made it," I thought; I could see the lights of Fort Colombo. "This way," I said, "I know the way now. Just a bit further. Run!"

The monsoon rain broke on our heads. Suddenly she stopped. I pushed her; she held on to me.

"What's up?"

"Blood."

I didn't understand.

"I'm bleeding, I tell you, idiot!"

I felt my sweat running; it was cold. "A lot?"

"A river."

The rain turned heavy and I put my jacket round her.

"Take your shirt off," she said.

I did it. She tore it quickly from top to bottom and moved away a little. By now the rain was coming down in buckets; I looked around helplessly. Fifty metres ahead loomed the big stone temple. Open day and night, for travellers, for people caught in the rain, hunted people, sick people, crazy people ... "Look," I said, pointing. "We'll go in there. Can you make it?"

"I can't walk a step. I'm in pain."

I picked her up and set off. She was light, but even so it wasn't easy. I took her in through the little open doorway and put her down on a stone bench. Pitch dark; smelt like a cave. The girl was breathing roughly. I lit my lighter; Catherine gave a wild scream. I saw there were three of us. The temple beggar was standing there: Salayia, my only friend in Colombo ... whenever I'd passed through the city, even if it was just for an hour, I'd always been to find her, to give her something. She called to me, by name. At that moment, if it had been my sister I'd seen standing before me I couldn't have been more pleased.

"We've made it," I said to the English girl.

"I'm dying," she moaned. Her hands were cold, her pulse barely perceptible.

"Wait," the old woman said to me. "Don't worry, I know."

She disappeared into the darkness. The girl started to cry; I held her hands.

The old woman crept back. "Be careful," she said. "Don't spill it. Make her drink it, quickly."

I gave Catherine the copper bowl; she drank thirstily.

"And this here," the old woman continued, putting something in my hand, "Goes down there. Right inside, deep."

"You do it, Salayia," I said. "Please."

"Me? Never. I can't. I'd be defiled for ever." She went a little way off and sat down.

"Give me your scarf," I said to Catherine.

"I threw it away; it was soaked."

Some time passed. Only the sound of the rain.

"How d'you feel?"

"Better. I think it's stopped." She tried to sit up. "Ah! my back hurts. Wait a bit."

I heard the beggar-woman's voice nearby. "Niko," she said, "Go over to Fort Colombo and bring two rickshaws. Ask for Fernando and Antonio: they were baptized by the Portuguese, they're your people."

"Don't go away," the Scots girl said, crying. "Don't leave me with this vulture. I'm scared of her, she'll hurt me."

"I'll sort you out. I'll spit on you," I thought as I set off. "I'll kick your arse, but let's get this over with first."

The rain had stopped. I was back in a quarter of an hour. Salayia was waiting outside the temple, Catherine too, a little way off ... I helped her into a rickshaw. "But I could go on foot now," she said, "I feel fine."

For a few seconds the old woman and I stood facing each other. I reached for her hands, but she pulled away. I took out a handful of money.

"You're unclean," she said, "As good as dead. I can't take anything from your hands. Never."

I left the money on the stone bench.

"Take it away from there. Nothing can make it clean."

"God bless you," I said.

I got into the rickshaw, watched her fade into the darkness. "Salayia," I shouted, "Thank you."

"Go to hell!"

Negri's office was open. Some members of the crew, our own people, were bartering with the barefoot pedlars.

"You hold my bag," she said, just before we reached the customs. A customs officer looked at me and burst out laughing. Suddenly I saw in front of me a little chap in khaki trousers, naked from the waist up, with a dripping wet green trilby on his head; a startling sight. I was standing in front of the mirror by the tourist office.

Once on deck we went our separate ways.

"She's made a scrap of Russian leather of you," the purser called; "Your legs are shaking."

I went to my cabin and sat down on the bunk. I was still holding her bag. I thought of taking it down to her, but changed my mind. I closed the door and opened the bag.

Inside was a bundle of high-denomination notes and three rolls of lower value ones. Forty-five gold St Georges, the ones with the spear in his hand. And in a transparent folder the photograph of a huge Maori holding a fishing net.

Androyannis brought me my jacket during the afternoon watch.

"Give me her bag," he said.

"Why doesn't she come and get it herself?"

"She's in her cot. Didn't get up at all. Beautiful today; radiant."

"Why doesn't she get up?"

"Got a bit tired yesterday evening. You wore her out, she says. Tell me, mate ..."

"Another time. Did you take her any food?"

"Just now ... she's eating a lot; chewing away like a sheep since morning. She gave me a box of chocolates. I opened it; all melted with the heat. Told her. 'So what?' she says; 'Not my fault.' Well brought up; like a swineherd ... seems her period started today."

"Did she ask you for anything?"

"No. But not getting up ... want some pineapple?"

"Later."

"Shall I tell her anything?"

"Just say hello from me."

In the evening I saw her dancing with an American gigolo in a fancy shirt. Midnight she came up to me on watch.

"Hallo, Nick."

"Hallo. Sit down."

She came up close: "Kiss me."

I kissed her on the cheek; she smelt of youth.

"Is that how they kiss where you come from?"

"Yes; their sisters."

"What? We did really well yesterday. Only you were afraid."

"Yes, a little."

"A little? You should have seen your face when the Indian slipped over. As if it were your own leg that had got twisted."

"And how was it he fell down?"

"How should I know? I couldn't work it out."

"Go back to bed. Quickly."

"I'm not sleepy."

"Then go away from here; I've got work to do."

She looked at me doubtfully. I turned on the transmitter and called Colombo. When I'd finished she was gone.

For five days we didn't speak. The day we were due at Aden she came and found me: "Shall we go ashore together?" she asked.

"I don't know. I'll be busy."

In the evening as I was out walking by the oily rocks round Steamer Point, Dionysis from Karavado, who used to do a bit of smuggling, stopped me: "I'll be coming with you," he said. "Got back from Calcutta yesterday. You'd better go over to Photis's place right away, there's an English girl making a nuisance of herself, looking for you."

I took a car to go to Sheikh Othman; there were beautiful young black girls there. On the way I stopped at a shop to buy some beads, and when I got back in the car there was the Scots girl, crouched in the corner.

"Am I in the way?"

"No ... but I'm going out to a village, I've got something to do."

"I'll come too."

"All right, but you'll have to wait in the car."

"That's fine."

We reached the place. I was gone about a quarter of an hour ... it was dark by the time I got back to the car. As we set off, a young woman came running up with my scarf and lighter.

We set off in the direction of Steamer Point. Neither of us spoke. Outside the Crescent Hotel Catherine told the driver to stop. She opened the door a little and started to get out.

"Come with me," she said.

"I've got things to do."

"I know I haven't behaved well," she said, "But it was your fault too."

"Behave however you like," I said; "You'll come out on top for sure."

"I want to talk to you."

"I don't."

"You'll be sorry."

"Go away."

"All right, I'm going."

She got out and stood on the steps of the square; her eyes were flashing.

"Let's go," I told the driver.

"Slave!" she shouted as we drove away; "Servant!"

The next afternoon we were off to Abou Zabal, the Khamsin filling our mouths with sand. Androyannis came up to the wireless cabin carrying a flat box.

"Did she send you a telegram?" he asked.

"Who?"

"The English girl. She didn't want to wake you up in the night. She came around dawn and collected the silk she'd bought. She said Cory's office had orders for the *Himalaya* to wait for her; it's passing through today. She left me this for you. I'm off."

I opened the box ... a white nylon shirt.

To Grigoris Bekakis.

Diamantis gets up and puts on his shirt. His companion is walking up and down rubbing his eyes, stamping his leg that's gone to sleep. He looks at his watch; quarter past one. The ashtrays are full. He opens the window and a cloud of smoke billows out. Leaning out he sees the two coolies sitting back to back, smoking. He's getting goose-flesh from the humidity.

"Diamantis, give me your cigarettes."

"I finished them."

The door opens and the doctor comes in holding an envelope. "Are you fed up?"

"Oh, it doesn't matter. How much do we owe, doctor?"

"Nothing."

"That can't be."

The doctor pats Diamantis's shoulder; "I said 'Nothing.' You can go now. Bon voyage."

"Was she beautiful?" the wireless officer asked suddenly, pointing at the door of the other room.

The doctor took a passport out of his tunic pocket and handed it to him, open.

He took it. His eyes widened and his jaw dropped: "Melousine!" ... he dropped the passport and went out, holding his head in both hands. Diamantis, troubled, followed him.

Doctor Ma Tuan leant over the wooden banister and said gently "I'm not to blame. You asked. I'll see you again."

The coolies got up, and the wireless officer went over to the older one.

"Well tell me, then," Diamantis was pleading; "Give me the envelope."

"We're going now, we're late." He got into the rickshaw.

Diamantis pulled at his sleeve.

"When we get there."

The rickshaws set off. After a little way they drew alongside each other: "Yes or no?" shouted the cadet.

His friend put the envelope in his back pocket and didn't reply.

They reached the town, and started going through the narrow streets with their little red lights. A woman came out into the middle of the road and stopped the rickshaws; they got out. She was wearing a black kimono with red embroidery and gold and silver birds that flashed in the street lights. She was holding an oil-lamp with three wicks.

The wireless officer took the cigarette out of her mouth and drew on it; she laughed. The coolies had been paid off, but they didn't leave, just stood a few paces off. The woman's eyes looked around her from within a carapace of white and yellow make-up. She opened a door beside them and another woman appeared; she beckoned them.

"I want to go back to the ship," the cadet whined, "But tell me first."

The woman took both of them by the hands. There was a noise of women screaming and shouting from the corner; the two women and the coolies ran off. Aeroplanes were coming over, dropping flares.

They ran over to where the shouting was coming from and saw a group of half-naked Chinese women trying to drag a huge bundle through a narrow doorway. They dumped it outside and ran off.

The two of them bent to look. "It's Captain Panayis!" said the cadet, reaching down to pull open the shirt. The other felt the forehead and the pulse. Just then the siren of the *Pytheas* started to sound.

"He's cold— he's gone. Take him by the feet," the wireless officer said to the cadet. They dragged him into the square, which was full of soldiers. Aeroplanes came down low, shooting. Further off others were dropping bombs. People ran backwards and forwards chaotically.

They put him down, and Diamantis cupped his hands to shout "Anyone from the Greek ship ... Boys ..."

Bullets hit the ground nearby, then suddenly all was silent.

"Come on, Diamantis— you take his feet."

They were stopped by two soldiers with pistols in their hands: "Killed?"

"No, from the ship— heart attack."

"Follow us to the Health Inspectorate."

"No, we've got to take him with us, we're leaving, give us a hand."

"To the Health Inspectorate!" shouted the Chinaman, waving his pistol.

There was the sound of an aeroplane coming back and the two soldiers ran off.

The wireless officer bent down and closed the old man's eyes. With difficulty he pulled a ring off a cold finger; the ruby flashed as he handed it to the cadet: "Look after that." As he got up, a white enveloped slipped from his back pocket and fell in the mud.

"Now. Courage!"

They had to stop every few paces to get their breath. Mud to one side, rocks to the other. Once Captain Panayis slipped from their hands and crashed to the ground.

They crossed the wooden bridge and reached the jetty: the *Pytheas* had cast off all its hawsers but one. Only the rope-ladder hung from her side.

"Chose a good time to go after whores," shouted the Captain from the bridge. "Get up as best you can; we're off."

They put him down and stood there panting, their arms hanging loose.

The First Mate leant over the rail: "What's up? Come on, hurry! ... What's that you've got with you?"

"Captain Panayis. Come down. Set up the gangplank or throw down a line."

"Captain P ..." the First Mate said hoarsely. He stepped onto the rope-ladder and jumped down; bent over the body.

"Has he been bit?"

"No."

"He's cold already ... Panayis, you poor old sod ..."

The gangplank came down, screeching. The Captain and the Chief Engineer came ashore, behind them the steward, holding a box.

"Is he breathing?" asked the Captain.

"He's gone," said Yerasimos.

"Did you get a paper? Has a doctor seen him?"

No-one answered.

"Chose a good time, the Christian," said the engineer.

"The law says we should leave him," said the Captain, and looked at the engineer.

"Yes," growled the First Mate. "For the crows. Shit on the law."

"Two sailors down here," shouted the Captain.

"Nobody come down," said the First Mate. "The two of us'll take him up; let's not waste time."

Without a word, the Captain bent his vast bulk and took the dead man's feet. Yerasimos took the other end. They stumbled on the treads of the gangplank as they went up. Above them the sailors of the watch leant over, murmuring to each other.

They laid him on the hatch of the main stoke-hold.

"A little water," gasped the Captain, breathing heavily, "My lungs are bursting."

"Get a new tarpaulin," ordered the First Mate. "We'll keep him covered till we reach open sea."

"How the devil will we get out with no harbour lights, no pilot?" said the Captain. "This gutter of a harbour ..."

"No lights to show on the ship. Diamantis will take the eight to twelve on his own, and Captain Pantelis the old man's watch."

"Yes," said the Captain softly, "And who's going to untie the hawsers?"

"There are two people talking on the jetty. Let's go up."

The telegraph rang like a church bell.

"Weigh anchor!"

"Loose the lines!"

The bows of the *Pytheas* swung out to port. On shore, two women in evening gowns lifted the hawsers from the bollards, then took off their shawls to wave.

Melbourne 15.8.1951 s.s. Cyrenia.
Tyrrhenian Sea 21.12.1952 s.s. Corinthia.

Glossary

Aldis
The Aldis lamp throws a powerful beam which can be interrupted rapidly by means of shutters in front of its lens. It is used for signalling in Morse code.

Apocalypse
The quotation is of course from the Greek version; I cannot find it in the Authorized version.

Baklava
A kind of sweet, sticky cake.

Barbar
Slang for "Uncle"; a friendly but respectful form of address to an older man.

Bones
It is the Greek Orthodox custom to disinter bodies after three years or so. The cleaned bones are put in a box to be stored in an ossuary, preferably in the deceased's home village.

Breakages
Greeks sometimes like to make a display of wealth by deliberately breaking plates etc. in tavernas, indeed in some establishments, known as "Sky-ladikos", ("Dog-places") it is expected behaviour.

Burial-offerings
A ritual offering of sweetened boiled wheat.

Captain
All officers in the Greek Merchant Marine are known informally as "Captain".

Cement broken in the hawse-pipes
The hawse-pipes are the holes in the bows through which the anchor-chains run. They were often blocked with cement on long voyages, to keep heavy seas out.

Christian
Greeks often say "The Christian" where we might say 'The chap' or 'The fellow'.

Contageous	Where the original text is in languages other than Greek – wireless messages, for instance, are given in English – I have usually retained Kavvadias's spelling etc.
Feast of St Nicholas	Patron saint of sailors. As Greeks celebrate name-days rather than birthdays, a doubly significant day for Nikos.
First Dog	The original title *Vardia* translates as "Watch" in the sense of ship-board vigil. The intriguing title "First Dog" was suggested (over a suitably naval pink gin) by Alan Ross. Watches are normally four hours long, but the dog-watch, from four to eight p.m., is divided into a "First dog" from four to six and a 'Last dog' ("Second dog" is a sole-cism) from six to eight. There are thus seven watches in a twenty-four hour day; seven being a prime number this arrangement helps ensure a fair rotation of duties.
Five Fingers	A gesture of thrusting the hand forward with palm outstretched; a gross insult to a Greek.
Fo'c'sle	Forecastle. In most Merchant Marines, the living quarters for lower ranks.
Loukoumi	What we know in England as Turkish Delight. A pretty girl is often likened to loukoumi.
Malaka	Literally "Wanker". The commonest of Greek insults.
Meltemi	Persistent north wind; the Greek equivalent of the Mistral.
Mema	Short for Yerasimos.
Metland	An unpopular British Governor in the Ionian Islands in former times. To invoke his name when cursing would indicate that one is from that area.
Midshipman	This is, in England, a rank in the Royal Navy, not the Merchant, where the equivalent is Cadet or Apprentice. Something similar obtains in Greece, hence Linatseros's wry comment on the Third Officer's lost love.

Narghilé	Bubble-pipe. In former years these were available in cafés, where regular customers might keep their own private one.
Ouzeri	Place serving ouzo and the small snacks that usually accompany it.
Put the eye on us	Even today many educated Greeks believe in the Evil Eye.
Rat Guards	These are the conical objects often seen on ship's hawsers in dock. They prevent rats entering or leaving the ship by this route.
Saint Vasili's Day	New Year. In Greek tradition presents are exchanged on this day rather than at Christmas.
Scorpion-fish	An ugly red bottom-feeding fish, common in the Mediterranean and prized for its soup-making potential. So called for its many spines, which can give a painful sting until the fish is cooked.
Sigri	The westernmost port in Mytilene. (Lesbos).
Snakes and a singleside	An attempt at a literal translation of a bizarre Kephallonian curse.
Springs	Long mooring-lines, one running from the stern to a point on the jetty forward of the ship, and another running from the bows to a point on the jetty aft of the ship, acting as shock-absorbers in heavy seas.
Syntagma and Omonia	The two main squares of central Athens.
Webster	I have given the epigraph from *The Duchess of Malfi* exactly as it appears in the Greek original, complete with minor errors.

OTHER BOOKS FROM SHOESTRING PRESS

MORRIS PAPERS: Poems Arnold Rattenbury. Includes 5 colour illustrations of Morris's wallpaper designs. "The intellectual quality is apparent in his quirky wit and the skilful craftsmanship with which, for example, he uses rhyme, always its master, never its servant." *Poetry Nation Review.*   ISBN 1 899549 03 X   £4.95

INSIDE OUTSIDE: NEW AND SELECTED POEMS Barry Cole. "A fine poet ... the real thing." *Stand.*   ISBN 1 899549 11 0   £6.95

COLLECTED POEMS Ian Fletcher. With Introduction by Peter Porter. Fletcher's work is that of "a virtuoso", as Porter remarks, a poet in love with "the voluptuousness of language" who is also a master technician.   ISBN 1 899549 22 6   £8.95

STONELAND HARVEST: NEW AND SELECTED POEMS Dimitris Tsaloumas. This generous selection brings together poems from all periods of Tsaloumas's life and makes available for the first time to a UK readership the work of this major Greek-Australian poet. ISBN 1 8995549 35 8   £8.00

ODES Andreas Kalvos. Translated into English by George Dandoulakis. The first English version of the work of a poet who is in some respects the equal of his contemporary, Greece's national poet, Solomos.   ISBN 1 899549 21 8   £9.95

LANDSCAPES FROM THE ORIGIN AND THE WANDERING OF YK Lydia Stephanou. Translated into English by Philip Ramp. This famous book-length poem by one of Greece's leading poets was first published in Greece in 1965. A second edition appeared in 1990.   ISBN 1 899549 20 X   £8.95

POEMS Manolis Anagnostakis. Translated into English by Philip Ramp. A wide-ranging selection from a poet who is generally regarded as one of Greece's most important living poets and who in 1985 won the Greek State Prize for Poetry. ISBN 1 899549 19 6   £8.95

SELECTED POEMS Tassos Denegris. Translated into English by Philip Ramp. A generous selection of the work of a Greek poet with an international reputation. Denegris's poetry has been translated into most major European languages and he has read across the world. ISBN 1 899549 45 9   £6.95

THE FIRST DEATH Dimitris Lyacos. Translated into English by Shorsha Sullivan. With six masks by Friedrich Unegg. Praised by the Italian critic Bruno Rosada for "the casting of emotion into an analytical structure and its distillation into a means of communication", Lyacos's work has already made a significant impact across Europe, where it has been performed in a number of major cities.   ISBN 1 899549 42 0   £6.95

A COLD SPELL Angela Leighton. "Outstanding among the excellent", Anne Stevenson, *Other Poetry.*   ISBN 1 899549 40 4   £6.95

BEYOND THE BITTER WIND: Poems 1982–2000, Christopher Southgate. ISBN 1 899549 47 1   £8.00

SEVERN BRIDGE: NEW & SELECTED POEMS, Barbara Hardy.
ISBN 1 899549 54 4   £7.50

WISING UP, DRESSING DOWN: POEMS, Edward Mackinnon.
ISBN 1 899549 66 8   £6.95

CRAEFT: POEMS FROM THE ANGLO-SAXON Translated and with Introduction and
notes by Graham Holderness. Poetry Book Society Recommendation.
ISBN 1 899549 67 6   £7.50

TOUCHING DOWN IN UTOPIA: POEMS, Hubert Moore
ISBN 1 899549 68 4   £6.95

WAITING FOR THE INVASION: POEMS, Derrick Buttress
ISBN 1 899549 69 2   £6.95

HALF WAY TO MADRID: POEMS, Nadine Brummer
ISBN 1 899549 70 6   £7.50

GIFTS OF EGYPT: POEMS, Michael Standen   ISBN 1 899549 71 4   £7.95

THE ISLANDERS: POEMS, Andrew Sant   ISBN 1 899549 72 2   £7.50

COLLECTED POEMS, Spyros L. Vrettos
ISBN 1 899549 46 3   £8.00

FIRST DOG Nikos Kavvadias. Translated into English by Simon Darragh
ISBN 1 899549 73 0   £7.95

TESTIMONIES: NEW AND SELECTED POEMS Philip Callow. With Introduction by
Stanley Middleton. A generous selection which brings together work from all periods of the
career of this acclaimed novelist, poet and biographer.   ISBN 1 899549 44 7   £8.95

PASSAGE FROM HOME: A MEMOIR Philip Callow. Angela Carter described Callow's
writing as possessing "a clean lift as if the words had not been used before, never without its
own nervous energy."   ISBN 1 899549 65 X   £6.95

Shoestring Press also publish Philip Callow's novel, BLACK RAINBOW.
ISBN 1 899549 33 1   £6.99

For full catalogue write to:
Shoestring Press
19 Devonshire Avenue
Beeston, Nottingham, NG9 1BS UK
or visit us on www.shoestringpress.co.uk